ALEX AND PENNY

BALLOONING OVER ITALY

This book belongs to

THE MAIN CHARACTERS IN THIS BOOK ARE

PENNY LIKES

snorkeling with a mask and fins

playing with her kitten

sketching and reading art books

PENNY DOESN'T LIKE

dressing up for dinner at her aunt and uncle's house

big spiders

doing math homework

WHAT DO YOU LIKE?

List three things you like and three things you don't...

1) ....

2) ....

3) ....

PENNY AND ALEX

ALEX LIKES

challenging his friends to daring skating races

reading stories set in outer space

playing computer games and surfing the Web

ALEX DOESN'T LIKE

cleaning his room

the smell of lima beans

getting up early in the morning

WHAT DON'T YOU LIKE?

Or, send them to us by email at: **alex@whitestar.it**
or: **penny@whitestar.it**

1) _____

2) _____

3) _____

Alex would never have expected it, but he had to admit it—

summer vacation had only just started, and he was already getting bored!

A few days ago, if anyone had told him this would have happened, Alex wouldn't have believed it. How can you get bored on vacation? As a matter of fact, the first days were unforgettable! No alarm rang to wake him in the morning, and when he got up, he would run straight to the beach and dive into the waves, build sand castles, and invent complex, and basically useless traps for crabs. Of course, in the beginning he missed his computer, but Alex soon found another source of fulfillment—his daily ice-cream challenge.

For days he had tested the patience of the town's little old ice-cream man, asking for ever more absurd flavors and disgusting combinations. Unfortunately, even that hobby came to an end—Alex remembered with a shudder the small, smug smile plastered on the face of that little man as he offered Alex a new flavor invented for the occasion: broccoli! He had served it with almond praline and coconut, winning the game with a truly unique and gross combination! From that moment on, Alex had spent hours dozing on the beach, resigned to the fact that his vacation would no longer have any adventure in store for him.

And so it was, until…

"Alex! Alex, wake up! Did you read this?" Penny exclaimed.

"Whaaaaaa' haaaapaaaee' Wenny?" Alex mumbled, yawning.

He meant, "what happened Penny?" which he repeated as he lazily opened an eye and slowly turned his head until he glimpsed his sister's red ponytail sticking out from behind a newspaper.

WANTED: Urgently seeking individuals prepared to face daily risks and danger. Shrewdness and intelligence are necessary. Knowledge of history, art, and computers; curiosity; and experience solving mysteries also required.

Penny lowered her gaze and stared at her brother disapprovingly. Even though they were twins, you could never have found two more different people. For starters, Penny wasn't getting bored at all; of course, she loved a bit of adventure every now and then too, but she had finally found time to finish two books she had started months before, and to capture on her sketch pad a marvelous sunset and a funny-colored fish that she had seen while snorkeling. She couldn't stand how lazy Alex had become, but she knew that what she was about to tell him would quickly energize him.

"Alex! I can't believe it, you are falling back asleep! Wake up! Have you read this?"

"Who? What?" Alex asked.

"This ad. It's so strange! 'Urgently seeking individuals prepared to face daily risks and danger. Shrewdness and intelligence are necessary. Knowledge of history, art, and computers; curiosity; and experience solving mysteries also required.' Look, there's even a telephone number."

Alex sat straight up, suddenly awake and concentrating. "Penny, they're looking for us! We're perfect! For example, you have that strange obsession with art and history, and I am a wizard on the Web. I can do anything on computers, and as for shrewdness…well, I've got that, too."

Penny decided to let this last comment go. "And what about risk and danger?"

"What risk is there in calling that number and asking for more information?" replied her brother.

"Come on, let's call!"

Penny thought about it for a second, but couldn't find any reason to object and had to admit she was as curious as Alex.

A quick look between them was enough to make a decision; they got up and ran home to call. Alex dialed the number in the ad, and with their heads close together and the receiver in the middle, they waited for someone to answer.

"Hello?" they heard someone whisper.

"Um, hello…I'm calling about an ad I read in the paper today. You are looking for help…" began Alex.

"Shhhh! We mustn't talk on the phone, it's not safe! Meet me tomorrow morning at the Genoa Aquarium, in front of the dolphin tank. We can talk there!" Then the phone went silent.

"That call was even stranger than the ad! What should we do Alex? Alex?" Penny turned; and just one look at her brother's excited expression was enough for her to be sure that the next day they would show up for the appointment with the

mysterious voice.

GENOA

The next day, the twins got to Genoa on time, ready for adventure. As they arrived at the aquarium, Penny, watching Alex out of the corner of her eye, remembered her unbelievable wake-up that morning: Alex the Sleepyhead, that incredible lazybones of a brother—able to invent the worst tricks just to stay under his warm covers—had come whirling into her room like a tornado, ready to go and totally impatient! Alex had spent most of the night thinking about that odd ad; he was too excited to sleep and unable to stay still in his bed, so he got up at dawn and had been reading about Genoa and its aquarium for the last few hours.

"Alex, did you find any information about the city?" asked Penny.

"Lots. Genoa's history is over a thousand years old! Did you know that in the Middle Ages it was one of the four Maritime Republics, meaning, it was one of the four most powerful cities in the Mediterranean along with Venice, Pisa, and Amalfi? For decades, these rivals fought huge naval battles to dominate the sea. Cool, right?"

"*You*, interested in history? That *is* cool," answered Penny, laughing.

"Well, seeing as how you are having so much fun, little sister, here's another historical curiosity: Do you know who Genoa's most famous citizen of all time is? I'll give you a hint: He discovered a continent…by accident."

"Of course! Christopher Columbus! I know that story, too. Columbus was sure that the world was round like a ball even though he lived when everyone thought it was flat like a disc. He thought he could reach the Far East by sailing a few weeks west instead of taking the land route to the east, traveling the long and dangerous Silk Road. However, he never imagined that along that route he would find one small thing—America!"

"And what can you tell me about the aquarium?" asked Alex. "You are the expert on masks and fins, aren't you?"

"I read that it is one of the biggest aquariums in Europe. Dolphins, sharks, tropical fish, giant crabs, seals, and even penguins from Antarctica swim in enormous tanks," exclaimed Penny, hoping to have the time to sketch some of the rarer fish there.

8

DID YOU KNOW THAT…
In 1492, the rulers of Spain decided to help the Genovese explorer Christopher Columbus, loaning him three ships, called caravels, named Pinta, Nina, and Santa Maria. But, what neither the Spanish sovereigns nor Christopher had expected to find was…no less than a continent!

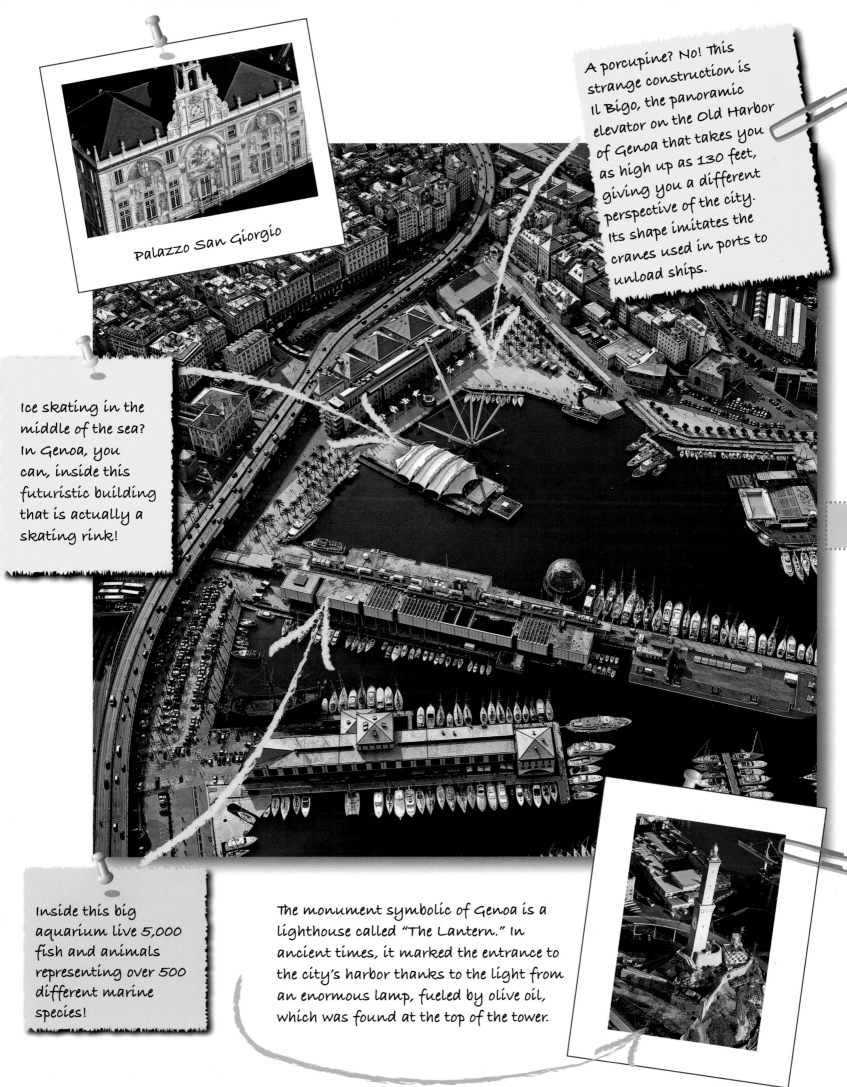

Palazzo San Giorgio

A porcupine? No! This strange construction is Il Bigo, the panoramic elevator on the Old Harbor of Genoa that takes you as high up as 130 feet, giving you a different perspective of the city. Its shape imitates the cranes used in ports to unload ships.

Ice skating in the middle of the sea? In Genoa, you can, inside this futuristic building that is actually a skating rink!

Inside this big aquarium live 5,000 fish and animals representing over 500 different marine species!

The monument symbolic of Genoa is a lighthouse called "The Lantern." In ancient times, it marked the entrance to the city's harbor thanks to the light from an enormous lamp, fueled by olive oil, which was found at the top of the tower.

Once they entered the aquarium, the twins went straight to the dolphin tank, where they had been instructed to wait. "Alex, how will we find the mysterious person who we talked to on the phone?" worried Penny.

"I wouldn't worry! I bet he will find us. We'll probably hear a voice suddenly whisper 'Hey, you two!'"

"Hey, you two!"

"Alex, I got it. You don't have to repeat yourself," Penny chastised.

"But, that wasn't me...."

The twins slowly turned around and saw behind them, half hidden by the lobster tank, a penguin! A talking penguin? "Hey, here I am!" Looking up, the twins realized with relief that what they thought they saw talk was actually the shadow of a person behind the penguin. As they drew closer, Alex was unable to hold back a hearty laugh when he saw who was hiding behind the mysterious voice: a boy, barely older than they were, dressed like an Eskimo in a big scarf and wool mittens, with red cheeks from the heat and sweat dripping into his eyes. "Shhh," insisted the boy, looking around nervously, "don't make so much noise! We mustn't be noticed by anyone!"

"Of course!" Alex answered, as he wiped away the tears he had shed from laughing so hard, "if you don't want to call attention to yourself, why walk around in the middle of summer dressed as if you were in a snowstorm?"

"You mean…you think that I'm wearing a bad disguise? If so, tell me! After all, I'm not a field agent, I'm a scientist, and I'm disguised as a worker at the penguin tank. It seemed like a good idea. I tried to follow the Agency's disguise instructions…."

"What agency?" interrupted Penny.

"Oh, no! I can't tell you that! You have to find out by yourselves! If you want to work for the Agency, you have to prove your acumen and craftiness."

"How?" asked Alex, who couldn't wait to prove himself.

"As all candidates do: The Agency will challenge you to find their headquarters. If you can get there, you will have proven to be the right people for…uh, no, I can't tell you that, either. You will have to follow the clues we have left for you. By solving the puzzles you find at each step, you will be able to proceed and get closer to your destination. Are you ready to leave?"

"Sure!" the twins answered in unison. "Can I ask you a question first?" Penny asked politely. "Who are you? And, why did the Agency send a scientist to explain to us what we have to do?"

"Oh! A perfectly good question! I'm Agent K and I'm an eighth-level inventor at the Agency. I almost forgot to tell you the reason I'm here! I have something for you: a fantastic prototype! A high-tech means of transportation, which will allow you to travel quickly, a wonder of science and technology! Actually, it is one of my inventions. Come on, it's outside. I'll show it to you."

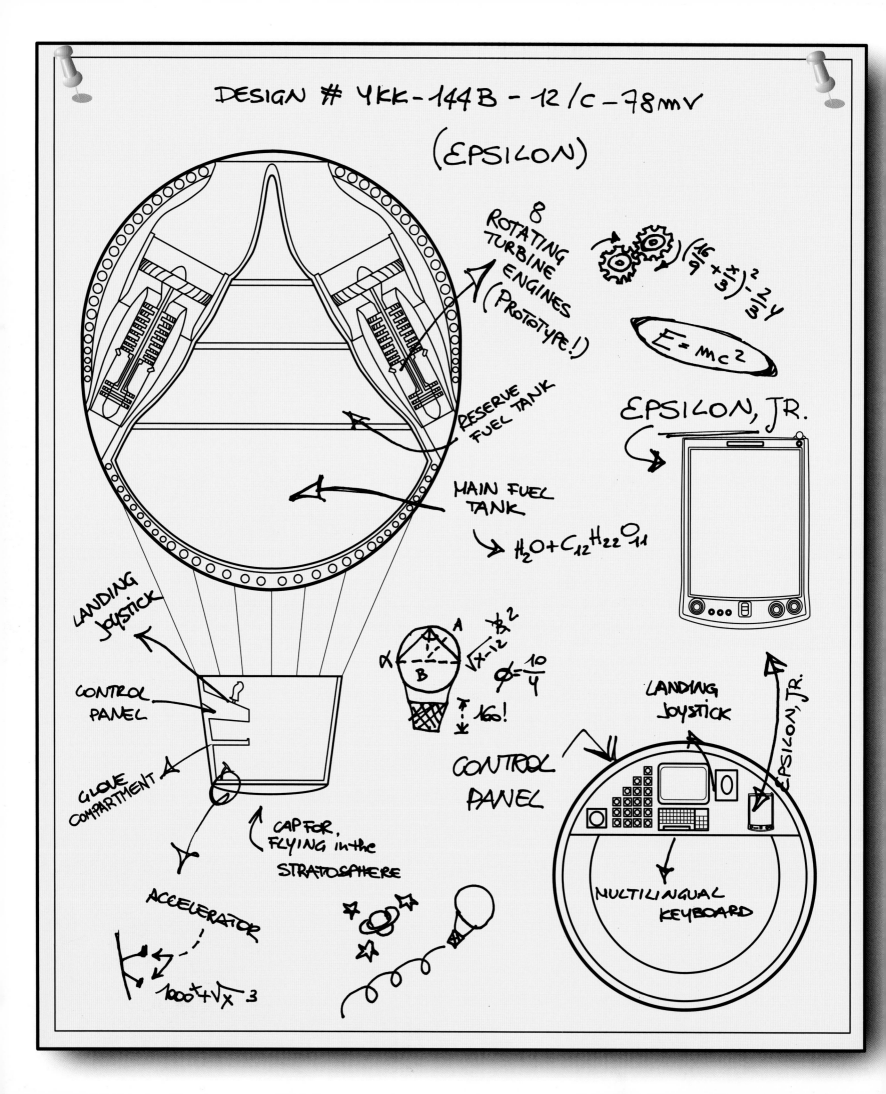

"A hot-air balloon?! This is your high-tech means of transportation?" Alex's voice expressed all the amazement and disappointment he felt. "I expected a supersonic jet, a space rocket, an atomic missile."

"It is all of that and much more! You are not looking at a simple hot-air balloon! What you are seeing is the prototype YKK-144B-12/c-78mV, but I affectionately call it Epsilon. It features eight rotating turbine motors that run on a new fuel I invented. I must say that it was a real stroke of genius to think of substituting the helium that propelled old hot-air balloons with a composite of H_2O and $C_{12}H_{22}O_{11}$."

"What?" the twins asked in unison. "What stuff is that?"

"Water and sugar, obviously," K answered looking at them. "Good idea, right?"

Alex and Penny glanced at each other, confused.

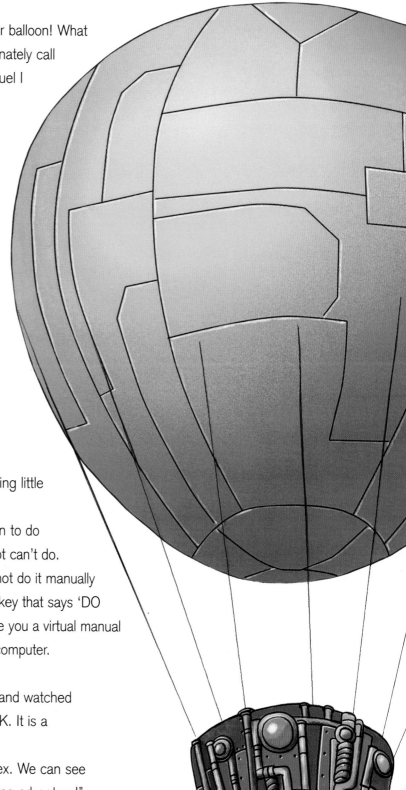

"Come on!" K called to them. "Look in the cabin. Here is the control panel. The on-board computer has a keyboard that makes it possible to write simultaneously in every language in the world, both past and present, just by pushing the purple button before typing the words. Handy, isn't it? See that instrument that looks like a little radio? It is a miniature portable computer! I call it Epsilon, Jr. You should keep it with you always because that's what we'll use to contact each other."

Alex was starting to get interested. Maybe Epsilon didn't look like a spaceship, but that hot-air balloon undoubtedly contained many intriguing little gadgets! "And that lever near the screen?" he asked.

K replied, "That's the joystick you have to use to land. You should learn to do that right away because landing is the only maneuver the automatic pilot can't do. Otherwise, remember that operating this gem is very complicated! Do not do it manually until you have learned the function of every button. And, don't use the key that says 'DO NOT TOUCH!' It is a secret device that I still have to fine-tune. I'll leave you a virtual manual with instructions. Your first destination is already programmed into the computer. So, what do you think?"

Alex got into the cabin, turned on the computer, grasped the joystick, and watched in amazement as dozens of glowing gauges and buttons lit up. "Wow, K. It is a fantastic invention!"

"And we can fly over all of Italy," cheered Penny. "Think how lovely, Alex. We can see everything from the sky, just like a bird. It'll be such a wonderful, exciting adventure!"

"So, what are we waiting for, sis? Let's go!"

TURIN

"We're here. This is our first stop: Turin."

"Are you sure, Penny? It is the first landing I'm trying, and I don't want to make any mistakes."

"We are in the right place, I'm sure. See that silver ribbon surrounding the city? It's the Po, the longest river in Italy, which originates in the Alps, not far from here, and crosses the entire plain of the Po River Valley until the Adriatic Sea…"

"But if it's so long, it must pass by many cities, not just Turin," objected Alex.

"I'm not done! Before you interrupted me, I was going to point out that dome down there."

"It's enormous! What is it?" asked Alex.

"It's one of the symbols of Turin. It's called the Mole Antonelliana because it was designed by the architect Alessandro Antonelli, in 1863. At 548 feet tall, it is the tallest stone building in Europe. Inside is the Cinema Museum and a big panoramic elevator that rises 279 feet in 59 seconds."

"Cool! Okay, let's begin the landing procedure! What else do you know about Turin?"

"It was founded by the Romans who called it Augusta Taurinorum, from which derives the modern name, Turin," continued Penny. "In the sixteenth century, it was the heart of the kingdom of the Savoy family, the same one that, in 1861, led the unification of Italy. That same year, Turin became the capital."

"Wait a second, the capital of Italy is Rome!"

"Turin was the first! Then, in 1864, the capital was moved to Florence, and Rome only became the capital in 1870."

"Cool! I didn't know that. Phew, we landed!" Alex said, "Now, we have to cross the city to get to the Egyptian Museum."

"Look at the map on your computer. Where are we?"

"I think Piazza San Carlo. There should be a statue on horseback."

DID YOU KNOW THAT… Ironhead is the nickname given to Emanuele Filiberto, the Duke of Savoy, in the sixteenth century, because he never wore a helmet, not even in battle. His statue stands in the center of Piazza San Carlo and is one of the symbols of the city.

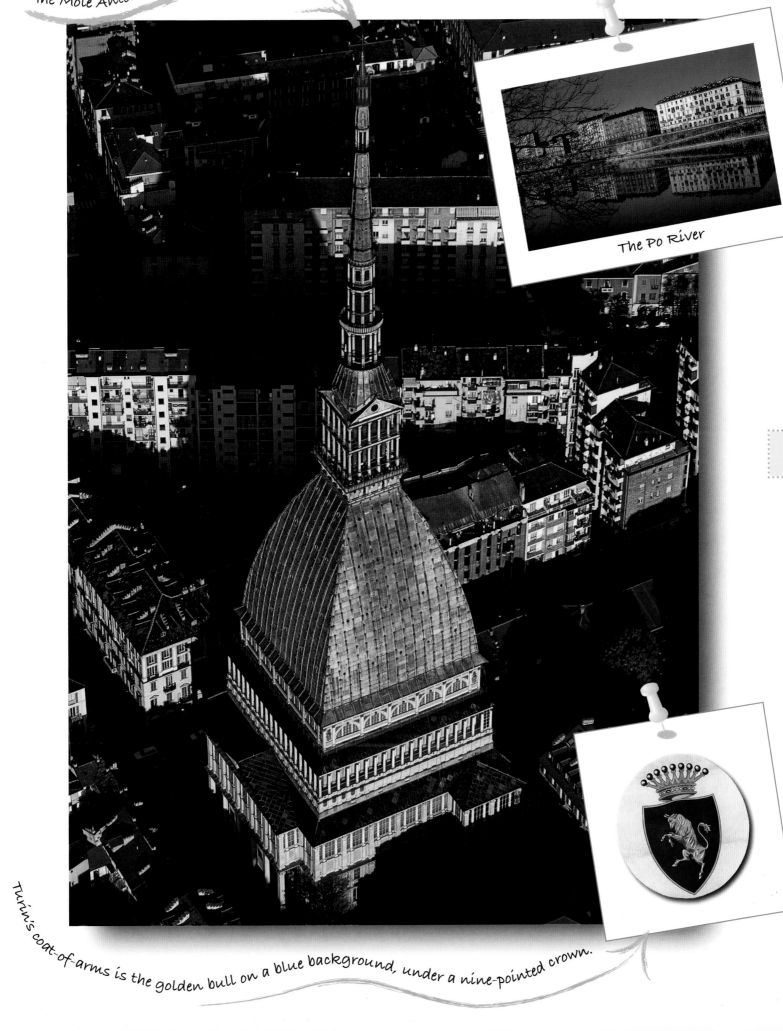

The Mole Antonelliana

The Po River

15

Turin's coat-of-arms is the golden bull on a blue background, under a nine-pointed crown.

THE CITY IS A LABYRINTH

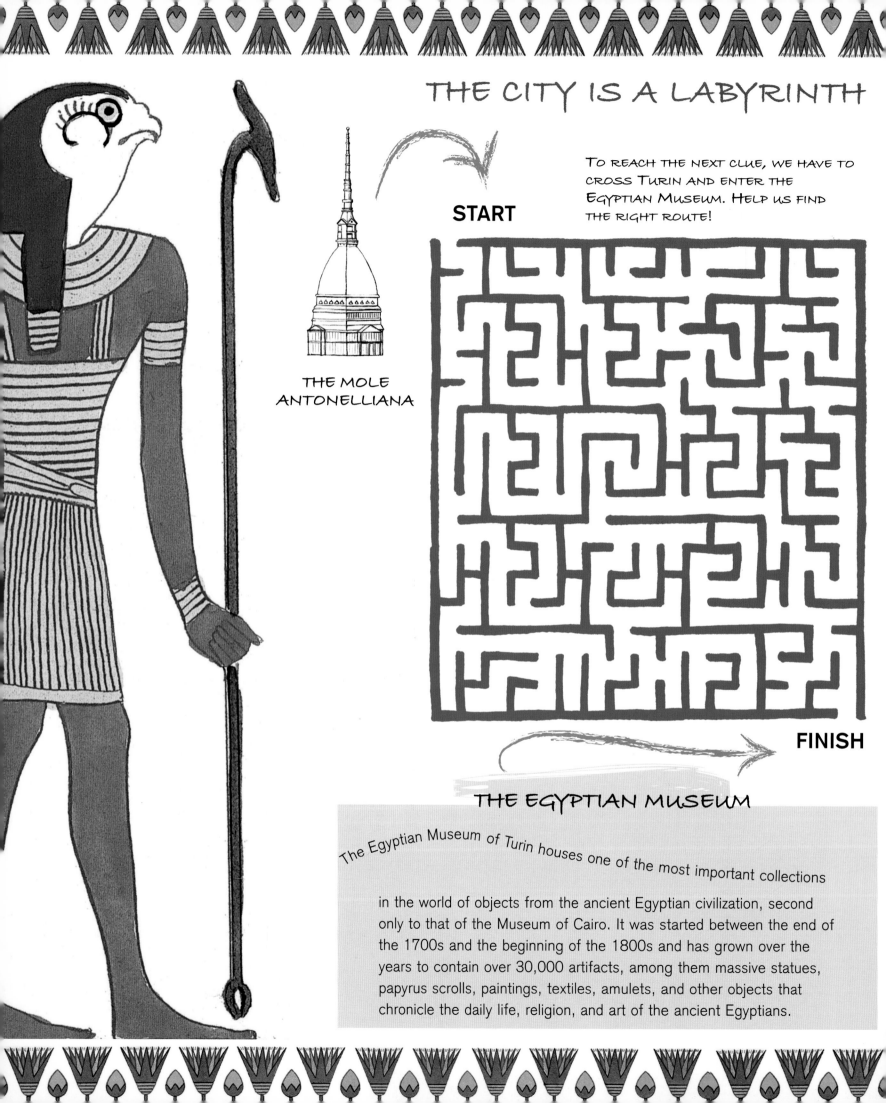

TO REACH THE NEXT CLUE, WE HAVE TO CROSS TURIN AND ENTER THE EGYPTIAN MUSEUM. HELP US FIND THE RIGHT ROUTE!

START

THE MOLE ANTONELLIANA

FINISH

THE EGYPTIAN MUSEUM

The Egyptian Museum of Turin houses one of the most important collections in the world of objects from the ancient Egyptian civilization, second only to that of the Museum of Cairo. It was started between the end of the 1700s and the beginning of the 1800s and has grown over the years to contain over 30,000 artifacts, among them massive statues, papyrus scrolls, paintings, textiles, amulets, and other objects that chronicle the daily life, religion, and art of the ancient Egyptians.

As soon as the twins entered the museum, they were amazed by the artifacts from the fascinating ancient Egyptian civilization. They would have liked to find the clue they needed to continue their journey quickly, but the more they looked around to find it, the more astonished they were by what they saw.

"Penny, look! That wig is more than 4,000 years old! And what is that? A comb! And look at those ancient sandals!"

"Did you see the colors in these hieroglyphics? I wanted to try to sketch them…." Penny's words were suddenly interrupted by Epsilon, Jr. which Alex had brought with him, as instructed by K. The small computer vibrated in his pocket, making him jump.

"Penny, you don't have time to draw anything. I got a message. 'Congratulations! We didn't expect you so soon. The clue you are looking for is behind the big statue of Ramses II. Do you know how to solve the puzzle it contains?'"

SOLVE THIS CLUE

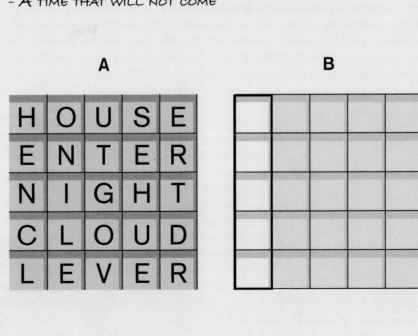

TO FIND THE NEXT STOP ON OUR JOURNEY, WE NEED YOUR HELP! WRITE THE ANSWERS TO THE RIDDLES IN TABLE **B**. FOR A HINT, CHECK TABLE **A**. EACH SOLUTION CAN BE FOUND BY CHANGING THE FIRST LETTER ON THE CORRESPONDING LINE IN TABLE **A**.
AT THE END OF THE GAME, YOU WILL SEE THAT THE SWITCHED LETTERS SPELL OUT THE NAME OF OUR NEXT DESTINATION.

RIDDLES

- IT LIKES CHEESE BUT HATES CATS
- IT MEANS TO "BURY"
- TURN ONE ON IF YOU CAN'T SEE
- YOU CAN READ TO YOURSELF OR YOU CAN READ …
- A TIME THAT WILL NOT COME

A

H	O	U	S	E
E	N	T	E	R
N	I	G	H	T
C	L	O	U	D
L	E	V	E	R

B

MILAN

In the cabin of the hot-air balloon, Alex studied the thousands of keys, levers, and buttons on the control panel. Mesmerized, he was trying to learn the meaning of every glowing gauge as quickly as possible and looking forward to the moment when he would finally be able to turn off the autopilot and fly Epsilon by himself. A green light suddenly lit up and began to flash, but Alex was not taken by surprise. After consulting K's instructions, he lowered a big red lever and read the words that appeared on the screen. "Sis, the computer says that we are arriving in Milan. Hey, did you hear me? Would you please tell me what you are reading that is so interesting?"

"A book on the history of the Duomo of Milan. Did you know that its construction was begun in 1386 and it has been going on ever since?"

"What? It has been under construction for more than 700 years?"

"Yes! Although there have been many interruptions in its building, many restorations, and alterations to the facade."

The computer screen on board flashed, and Alex read the new message aloud. "'The clue is at the base of the most famous statue in Milan.' Yikes! What statue could that be?"

"Alex, look!" The white spires of the Duomo were poking through the clouds, and Penny was pointing to the tallest spire, on which one of the symbols of the Lombard city sparkled in the sun—the golden statue of the Virgin Mary, the Madonnina.

"Alex, can we land over there? I think that is the statue we are looking for!"

The Madonnina stands at the top of the Duomo's tallest spire.

DID YOU KNOW THAT...

Visitors can take a steep old staircase or a modern elevator up to the roof of the Duomo. From there, they can enjoy a fantastic view of the city or wander through a maze of pinnacles; there are 135 in all, and each one is capped by a statue of a saint.

The facade of the Duomo

Penny was right again; the clue was waiting right at the feet of the golden statue! Alex was peering over the side of the balloon and grumbling while trying to think of a biting remark that would wipe away his sister's triumphant smirk when his gaze fell upon the imposing monument they were flying over—tall red walls, turrets, a moat…a castle in the middle of the city? "Penny, what is that?"

"I think it's Castello Sforzesco. I had hoped to see it. It's one of the most famous sights in the city. In 1300, the Visconti family built it outside the city walls, but then the city expanded and the castle was surrounded by the houses in what was like a full-on siege! In the fifteenth century, it was rebuilt by the duke of Milan, Francesco Sforza, and ever since then it has kept the name of 'Sforzesco.'"

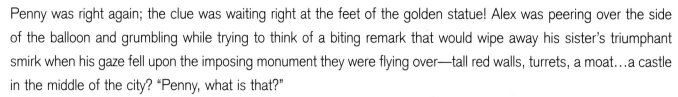

Francesco Sforza

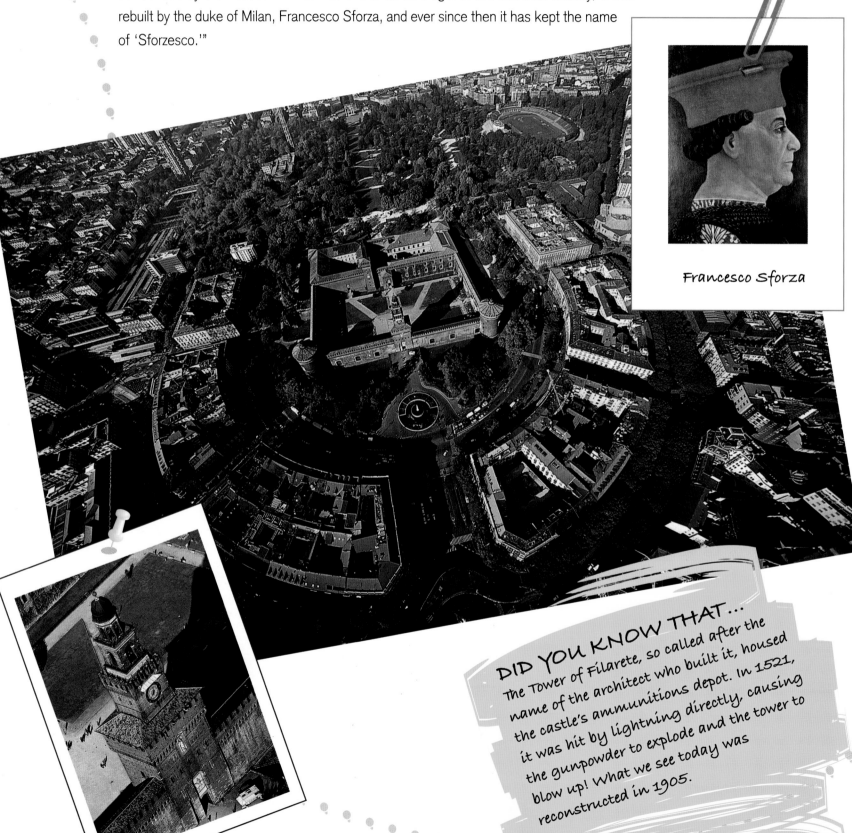

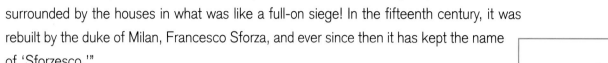

DID YOU KNOW THAT…
The Tower of Filarete, so called after the name of the architect who built it, housed the castle's ammunitions depot. In 1521, it was hit by lightning directly, causing the gunpowder to explode and the tower to blow up! What we see today was reconstructed in 1905.

ONCE UPON A TIME...

...a chef was so famous for his cooking ability that he was employed by the Lord of Milan to prepare a Christmas banquet for him and his court. The meal was delicious! The invited nobles showered every new dish with applause and at the end loudly called for the dessert. THE DESSERT? The chef realized that, overwhelmed by the preparations and the compliments, he had forgotten the dessert in the oven and now it was burned to a crisp—inedible! Hearing the chef wailing in despair, a young scullery boy named Tony approached him with a dessert he had made from some of the chef's leftover ingredients plus butter and candied fruits. The smell of the mixture was irresistible and the taste...delicious! The dessert was so successful that the chef decided to prepare it every year and call it, in honor of his young helper, Pane di Tony, meaning "Tony's bread."

PUT THE LETTERS IN THE CORRECT ORDER AND YOU WILL DISCOVER WHAT TONY'S BREAD IS CALLED TODAY.

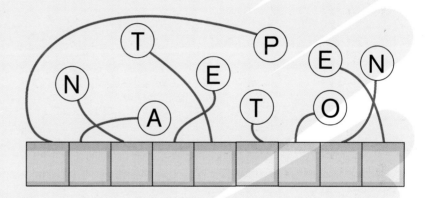

SOLVE THIS CLUE

FILL IN THE SQUARES WITH THE LETTER CORRESPONDING TO EACH SYMBOL TO DISCOVER ALEX AND PENNY'S NEXT DESTINATION.

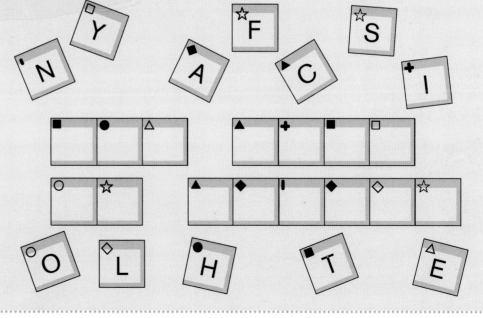

As we fly over St. Mark's Square, we can see the basilica, the bell tower, and the Ducal Palace.

The Doge dealt justice from the Ducal Palace.

The five domes on the Basilica of San Marco were influenced by the churches in Constantinople that Venetian merchants saw there.

VENICE

Alex leaned out of the balloon to get a better view of the thrilling spectacle they were flying over: the city of canals, Venice.

"Look, Penny. It really does look like a floating city. It's incredible! But why did they build a city on water?"

"I know why."

"Is there anything you don't know? Okay—tell me."

"After the fall of the Roman Empire…" began Penny.

"Zzzz…zzzz…zzzz"

"Alex! Don't pretend to sleep while I'm speaking! I hate that!" Penny protested.

"Okay, just this once I'll put up with your 'know-it-all' tone of voice. I'm too curious."

"As I was saying," continued Penny, "when the Roman Empire fell, peoples like the Visigoths, the Vandals, and the Huns of Attila were migrating to Italy. Some of them crossed the Veneto region, sacking the cities and threatening the country folk. The village inhabitants decided to take refuge in a swampy area near the sea and started to build their houses on the little islands in the lagoon.

Little by little, the islands were linked by bridges, and houses were built on tall stilts so people could live over the water. Within a few years, a real city had taken over the lagoon, and from those early floating houses, Venice was born."

"Phew! Now, let's land," exclaimed Alex. "Here's a new message. The next clue is between the paws of the Winged Lion in Piazza San Marco. Are you ready? We're going from a hot-air balloon to a gondola!"

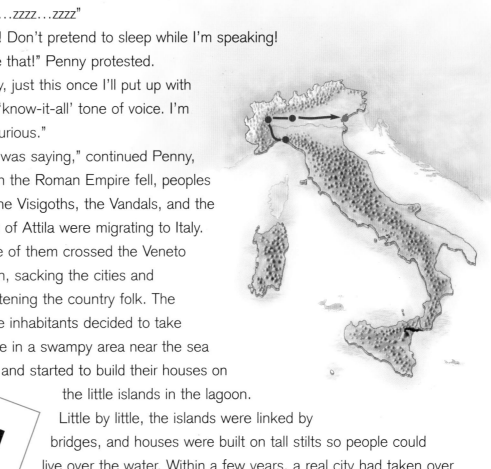

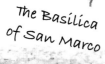

The Basilica of San Marco

START

HISTORIC REGATTA

The Historic Regatta is one of the oldest Venetian festivals. It has been celebrated every September for over 600 years! It is a fascinating festival that starts with a parade of historic boats led by the *Bucintoro*, the ancient ship of the Doge of Venice, covered with engravings and gilt and loaded with velvet. For one day, the Grand Canal is transformed into a racetrack for rowboats watched from the sides of the canals by thousands of spectators and fans.

FINISH

To look like a real gondolier, Alex has to wear their typical uniform—blue pants, a white sailor's sweater, and a straw hat with red ribbons.

THE CITY IS A MAZE

INSTRUCTIONS

WE ARRIVED RIGHT IN THE MIDDLE OF THE REGATTA, AND THE GRAND CANAL WAS PACKED WITH BOATS AND CROWDS. USING THIS DRAWING OF THE LAGOON, HELP US REACH PIAZZA SAN MARCO BY GONDOLA, TAKING THE SMALLEST CANALS, WHILE FOLLOWING THE BOATING RULES, TOO! PAY CAREFUL ATTENTION TO THE MAPS AND THE OBSTACLES BLOCKING THE CANAL!

KEY

 Gondola

 Under Construction

 No Entry

In ancient times, the Rialto Bridge was a drawbridge that opened in the middle to allow taller boats to sail down the Grand Canal. In 1588, it was rebuilt in stone with two rows of little shops covered by a portico.

25

This is a panoramic view of the lagoon from the balloon. It's gorgeous, isn't it, with that blue ribbon of water crossing the city and the Grand Canal?

PAX EVAN
TIBI GELI
MAR STA
CE MEVS

DID YOU KNOW THAT...

A lion with wings? The gilded statue doesn't portray an ordinary lion. Its wings represent St. Mark, the patron saint of Venice and the author of the Gospel, which the lion protects with its paw.

VENICE

30

1

29

27

26

25

28

2

4

5

3

6

8

7

24

9

THE VOYAGES OF MARCO POLO

It was 1271, and in Venice a boy was getting ready to take an incredible journey that would take him to the ends of the world as it was known at the time.
His name was Marco Polo. Marco left with his father and his uncle, merchants
and explorers, to visit the Far East and a mysterious land called Cathay. It was a
long voyage that allowed Marco to visit great cities; learn new languages and customs;
climb mountains; and cross deserts, meeting both fantastic and dangerous creatures in
those uninhabited lands. The Polos finally arrived at the court of the powerful and wise emperor of Cathay—Kublai Khan. The ruler listened to the tales that Marco told of their adventures
with interest. He was so impressed by Marco's powers of observation that he asked Marco to visit, as
his envoy, the most inaccessible places in his endless kingdom and to then report back about them to his court.
For many years, Marco traveled far and wide throughout Cathay, exploring the farthest reaches of the country until,
one day, he felt terribly homesick for his beloved Venice. Marco began the long journey home, bringing with him pre-
cious gifts from the emperor and, much more valuable than those, his memories of all the wonders he had seen. The
story of his adventures became one of the most famous books in the world, *The Travels of Marco Polo*.

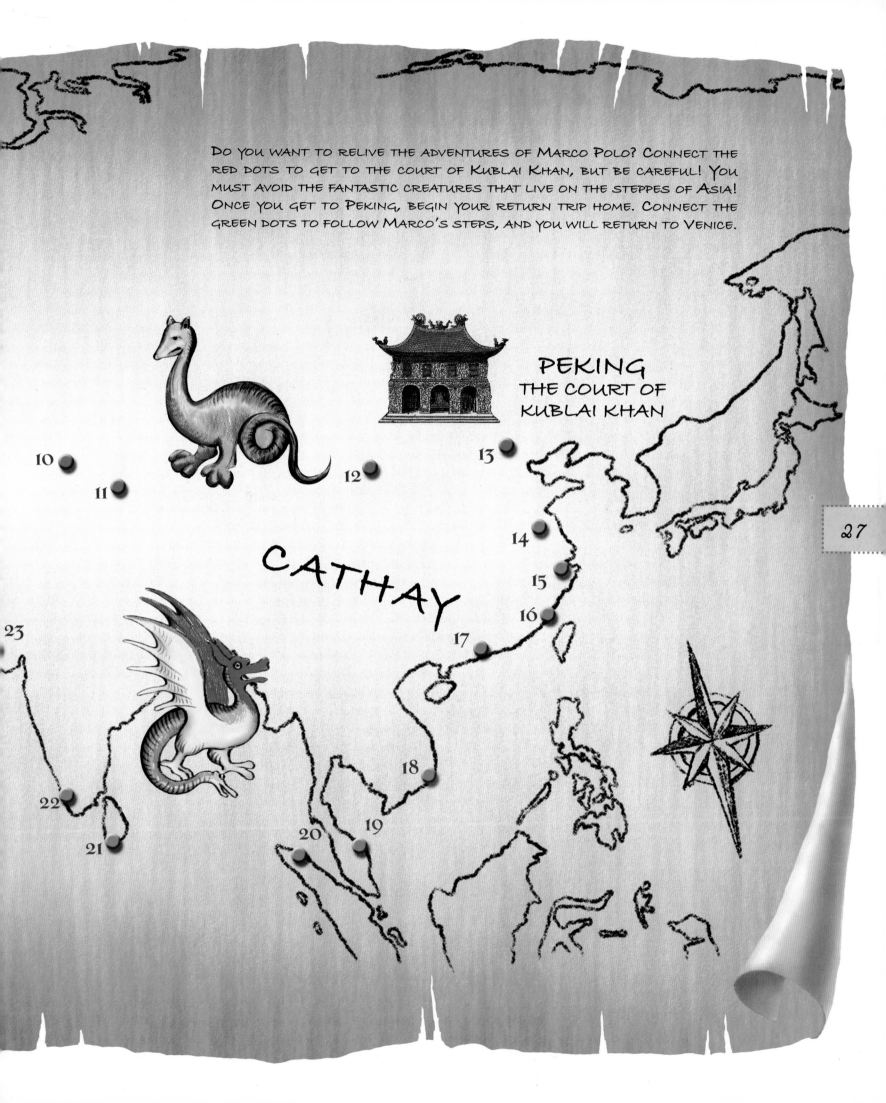

Do you want to relive the adventures of Marco Polo? Connect the red dots to get to the court of Kublai Khan, but be careful! You must avoid the fantastic creatures that live on the steppes of Asia! Once you get to Peking, begin your return trip home. Connect the green dots to follow Marco's steps, and you will return to Venice.

PEKING
THE COURT OF
KUBLAI KHAN

CATHAY

THE CARNIVAL OF VENICE

"Oh, Alex, it's so relaxing to ride in a gondola around the canals!" sighed Penny.

"Ugh! Ooof! Yeah, real relaxing," puffed Alex. "Mostly because I'm the one rowing, right?"

"Noooo, brother!" answered Penny, hiding a smile. "I was talking about this peaceful and picturesque atmosphere."

"You have to know, sis, that the picturesque atmosphere of the alleys and canals of Venice is overcome once a year by the most colorful and noisy festival in the world: Carnival! The relaxed city is overrun by masked people competing to be the most original. Here in Venice, Carnival is a serious affair, a centuries-old tradition. Just think that from 1400 to 1600, the art of the Mascareri and Tangheri, the makers of masks and papier-mâché shields, was located in this city!"

"Wait a second. Since when are you an expert on Carnival?"

"At Carnival, anything goes," exclaimed Alex, quoting a famous proverb. "Can you imagine a better holiday? Also, besides the most imaginative costumes, you can find some historic costumes in the streets, too. They can be easily recognized because their characteristics have remained the same for centuries.

"I know those, too! Harlequin is the lying and cunning servant who wears a suit in a thousand colors. Colombina is a mean little maid, a flirt, and a gossipmonger. The official costume of Venice is Pantalone, the old, grumpy, and greedy merchant. And now, let's go back to the balloon. We have a clue to solve."

COLOR IN HARLEQUIN, COLOMBINA, AND PANTALONE, CREATING A NEW COSTUME OR COPYING IDEAS FROM THE DRAWINGS ON THE OPPOSITE PAGE. THEN, INVENT A DIALOGUE THAT REFLECTS THE PERSONALITY OF EACH OF THE CHARACTERS.

SOLVE THIS CLUE

Help us figure out where our next destination will be. Cross out the letters on the wheel that spell the names of the three Carnival costumes: Harlequin (A), Colombina (B), and Pantalone (C). After that, read the remaining letters and you will know where Epsilon is headed next.

A

B

C

START

PISA

Every year, the tower leans another millimeter. This seems like a tiny amount, but every millimeter increases the risk that the tower will lose its unbelievable balance! Architects keep trying to find a way to prop up the tower.

"Do you have any idea how to find out where our next clue might be?" Hours had passed as Alex sat hunched over in a corner of the balloon with the computer on his knees, and Penny was starting to become really curious.

"I'll show you, sis. I looked up the 'Tower of Pisa' on the Internet, and I found thousands of results."

"I bet you did. It's one of the most famous monuments in the world!"

"Penny, listen to this. Did you know that it is called a tower but it's really a bell tower?"

"Oh! No, I didn't," Penny answered, amazed.

"What? You didn't know?! I said something my sister didn't know already? I can't believe it!"

"Must be the first time that has ever happened....Alex! Stop jumping around right now! We'll tip over."

"It's not possible. By now, I know this little gem of a balloon like the back of my hand!"

Piazza dei Miracoli, the Square of Miracles

"Alex, are you sure? Something's definitely not right!"

"Why do you say that?"

"Maybe it's because…the tower looks straight, but the rest of the square is now all tilted!" Alex looked out; it was true! The tower was straight, which hadn't been the case for centuries, but the rest of the world was now leaning to one side!

"Quick! Just push one of these buttons and then…oooops!"

Suddenly the balloon lurched, leaned to one side, rotated around, and dangerously rocked first to the right and then to the left. The twins ended up with their legs in the air on the other side of the cabin, while everything was shaking and creaking around them.

"Alex! What did you do?" shrieked Penny.

"Maybe I used the wrong lever, or maybe it was that button…wait! I know!" The vibrations immediately stopped, and a great silence descended upon them. Slowly, the twins looked over the side of the balloon and spotted the tower beneath them. It had gone back to being perfectly…tilted.

"Alex, you'll pay for this! Did you hear me?"

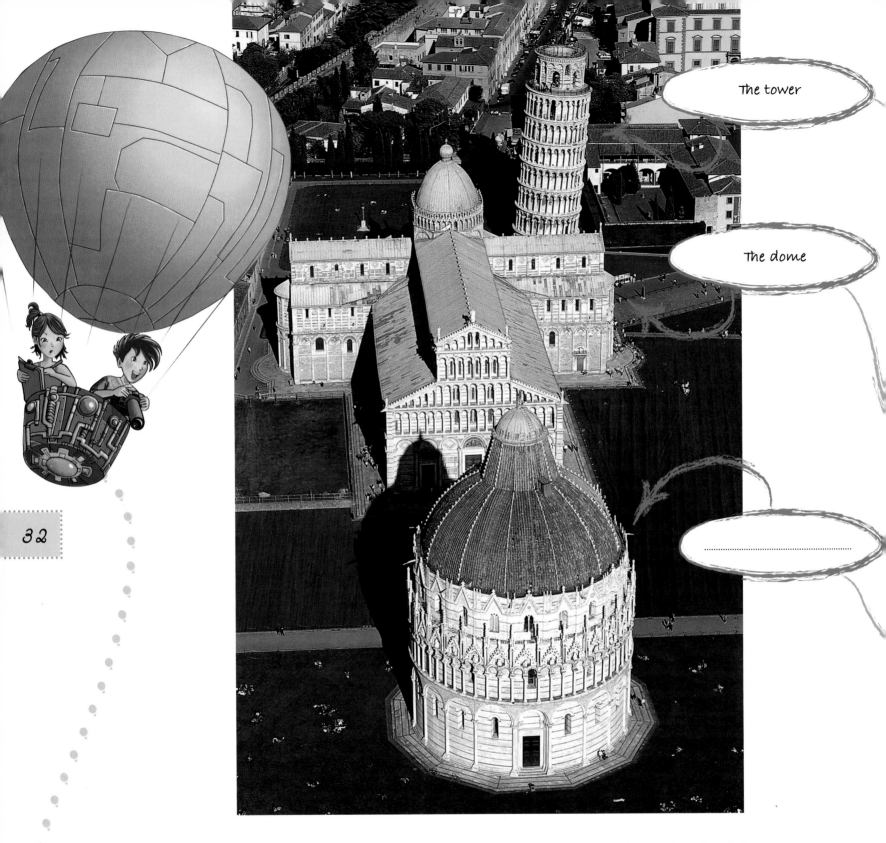

The tower

The dome

....

Penny's angry outburst was suddenly interrupted by a message on Epsilon, Jr. Alex hurried to read it with relief; for once, he would avoid being scolded. However, he found that he'd relaxed too soon...

"DIDN'T I WARN YOU THAT EPSILON IS VERY SENSITIVE? IT IS NOT A TOY! BE CAREFUL! And now, land. You have to get to the next clue. You have flown over Piazza dei Miracoli, where you will find, past the famous tower, two other important monuments: the Duomo, and the building where, in the Middle Ages, Pisa's citizens were baptized. The clue is hidden in the second building. Discover its name, and you will know where to go."

DISCOVER THE NAME OF THE THIRD MONUMENT

HELP THE TWINS DISCOVER THE NAME OF THE THIRD
MONUMENT. USE THE TERMS FROM THE LIST THAT AN
ART HISTORIAN WOULD USE WHEN SPEAKING ABOUT
THE MONUMENTS IN PIAZZA DEI MIRACOLI TO FILL IN
THE SQUARES BELOW. SOME LETTERS HAVE ALREADY
BEEN FILLED IN TO GET YOU STARTED. AT THE END OF
THE GAME, THE SHADED HORIZONTAL LINE WILL BE
FILLED IN WITH THE NAME OF THE MONUMENT!

TERMS

CATHEDRAL

GOTHIC

CHURCHYARD

SACRISTY

APSE

TOWER

MARBLE

CAPITAL

MIRACLES

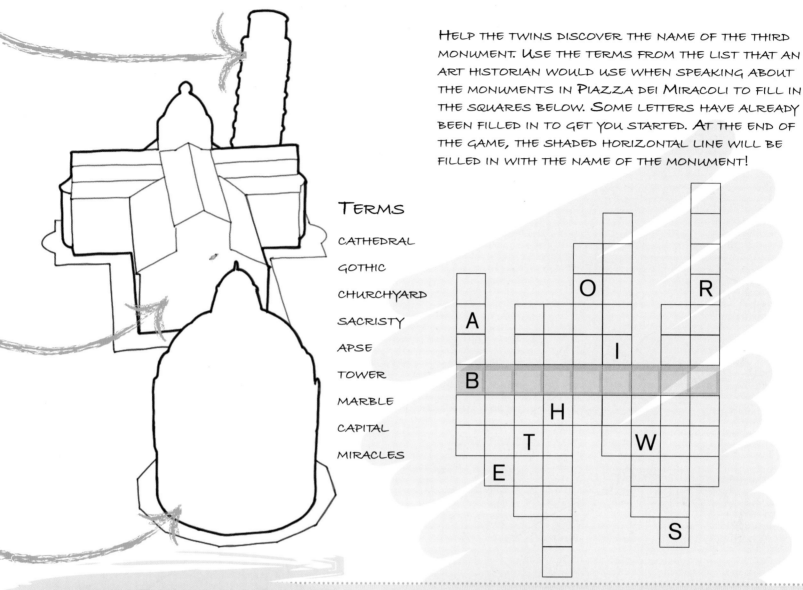

33

SOLVE THIS CLUE

SOLVE EACH OF THE SEVEN LITTLE RIDDLES AND
PUT THE ANSWERS IN THE APPROPRIATE SQUARE.
AT THE END OF THE GAME, YOU WILL KNOW
WHERE THE TWINS ARE GOING NEXT.

the first is the sixth letter of the alphabet

the fourth is in "roar" twice, in "roll" once, and never in "goal"

the sixth is the third letter in "Penny"

the second is the second letter in "Alex"

the third is in both "hot" and "cold" but not "warm"

the fifth is the same as the last

the eighth is in both "Alex" and "Penny"

the seventh is the third letter in the alphabet

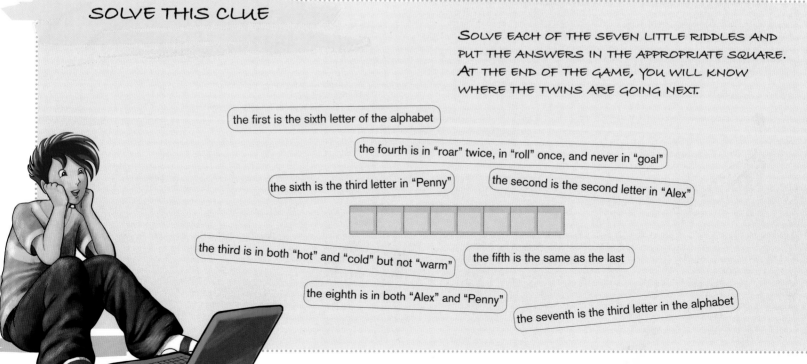

FLORENCE

"Florence! The home of the arts! Oh, Alex, I'm so thrilled! Do you realize that the masterpieces by the greatest artists that ever lived are right here? Michelangelo, Raphael, Botticelli, Brunelleschi..." Penny spoke without pausing for a breath as she continued to list the names of painters, sculptors, and architects. It seemed so unreal to her to finally be able to see all those masterpieces she had read about and tried so hard to copy on her sketch pad. Alex was looking at her, both amused and resigned; it was funny to see his sister, usually so calm, jump from one side of the balloon to the other, trying to glimpse Florence between the clouds!

"Penny, I haven't understood anything you've said. Calm down and start from the beginning!"

"Okay. I have a million things to tell you about the city."

"That's exactly what I was afraid of," sighed Alex.

"I'll start with its name. 'Florence' comes from 'Florentia,' the name the Romans chose when they founded the city. Do you know why they called it that?"

"No, but I'm sure you are going to tell me."

"In honor of Flora, the Roman goddess of spring, which was celebrated with games and festivals, precisely the period when they were looking for a name for the new city. We're here! Alex, we're here! That square down there is Piazza della Signoria. Do you know what really famous statue is found in front of Palazzo Vecchio, the 'Old Palace'?"

"The one that we are going to see now, I guess."

"Right," answered Penny with dreamy eyes, "the David by Michelangelo!"

DID YOU KNOW THAT...

Who was David? In the Bible, the story is told of young David who defeats the unbeatable giant Goliath armed with only a small slingshot. Michelangelo portrayed David with a slingshot held tightly in his fist and an expression of deep concentration on his face.

The Ponte Vecchio

Piazza della Signoria

A city called Florentia could only be represented by a flower, and as a matter of fact, the emblem of Florence has been a red lily for centuries.

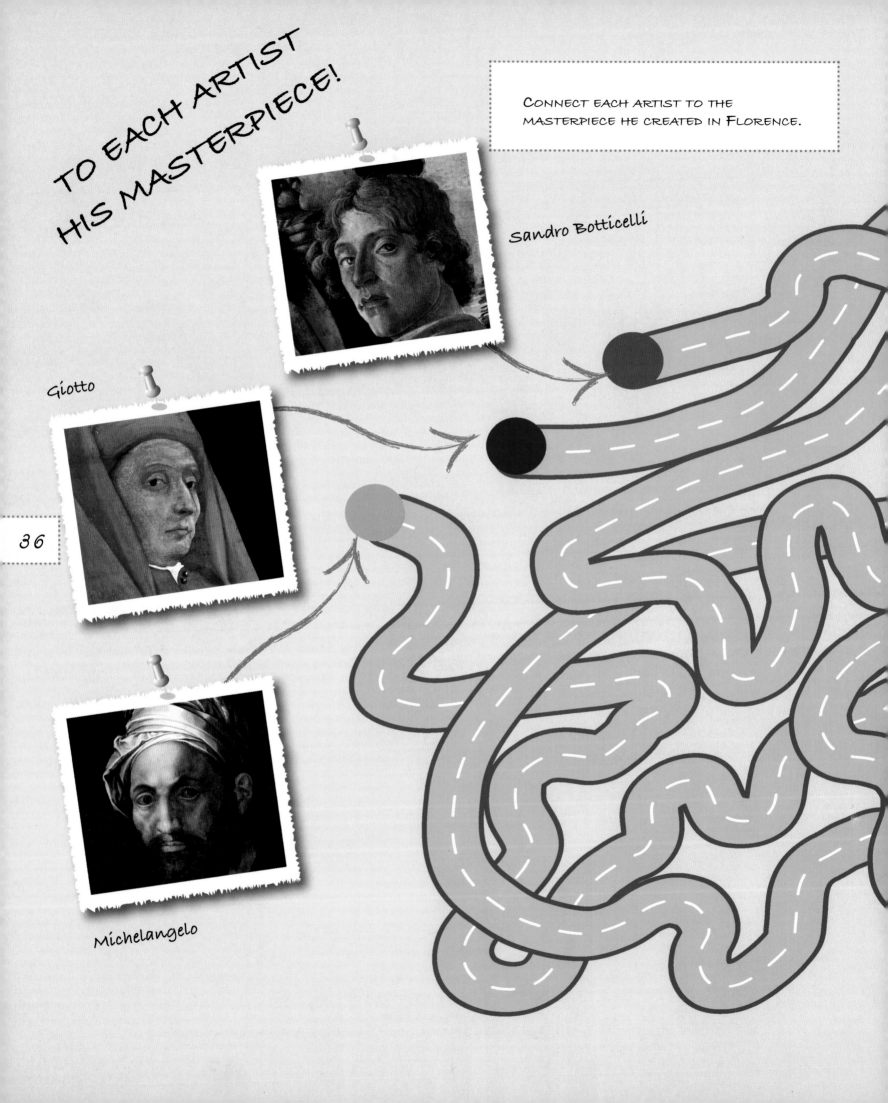

TO EACH ARTIST HIS MASTERPIECE!

CONNECT EACH ARTIST TO THE MASTERPIECE HE CREATED IN FLORENCE.

Sandro Botticelli

Giotto

Michelangelo

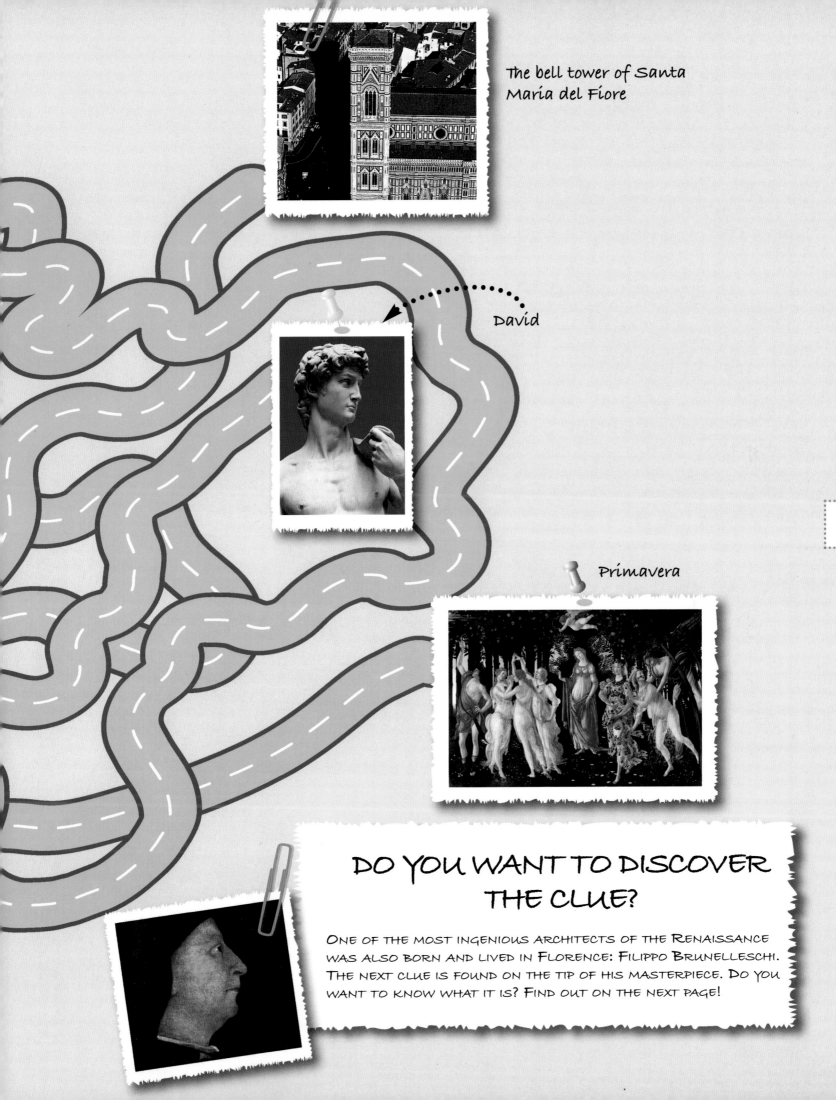

The bell tower of Santa María del Fiore

David

Primavera

DO YOU WANT TO DISCOVER THE CLUE?

ONE OF THE MOST INGENIOUS ARCHITECTS OF THE RENAISSANCE WAS ALSO BORN AND LIVED IN FLORENCE: FILIPPO BRUNELLESCHI. THE NEXT CLUE IS FOUND ON THE TIP OF HIS MASTERPIECE. DO YOU WANT TO KNOW WHAT IT IS? FIND OUT ON THE NEXT PAGE!

Filippo Brunelleschi's masterpiece is the dome of the Duomo, or cathedral, a record-breaking construction!

After discovering where the new clue was hidden, Alex and Penny jumped into the balloon to reach the big dome by air. Penny took advantage of the brief trip to tell her brother the story of its construction. "Think, Alex! Brunelleschi was inspired by ancient Roman and Eastern motifs, designing a building so magnificent that his peers, convinced he would fail, began to call him crazy. However, he didn't give up, and he designed machines able to lift the enormous weight of the bricks all the way up to the dome. He even worked out a special system to fit them together to make a truly sturdy structure. Many of his ideas were so innovative that his own workers didn't understand them, but Brunelleschi illustrated what he had in mind by using models of the dome that he built as he was speaking, with whatever material was at hand: damp soil, wax, or even a radish cut in half. In March 1436, the dome was finished and, in all of Florence, no one made fun of Brunelleschi's ideas anymore. Everyone agreed that he was an ingenious architect!

THE RECORD-BREAKING DOME

72 feet – the height of the top of the dome, called the Lantern.

108 feet – the height of the dome

37,000 metric tons – the incredible estimated weight of the dome

4,000,000 – the number of bricks used in its construction

SOLVE THIS CLUE

ON THE PUZZLE, CROSS OUT THE OBJECTS THAT YOU WOULD FIND IN A FLORENTINE PAINTER'S WORKSHOP, KEEPING IN MIND THAT THE WORDS CAN APPEAR ACROSS, UP, DOWN, OR BACKWARD. THE REMAINING LETTERS WILL SPELL THE NAME OF A FAMOUS RACE THAT IS HELD IN THE CITY THAT IS THE NEXT DESTINATION.

DRAWING - PICTURE - OIL - PAINT - PALETTE - PENCILS - FRAME - BRUSH

```
O P E N C I L S T
I F R A M E H E H
L G N I W A R D S
P A L E T T E P U
T N I A P A L I R
E R U T C I P O B
```

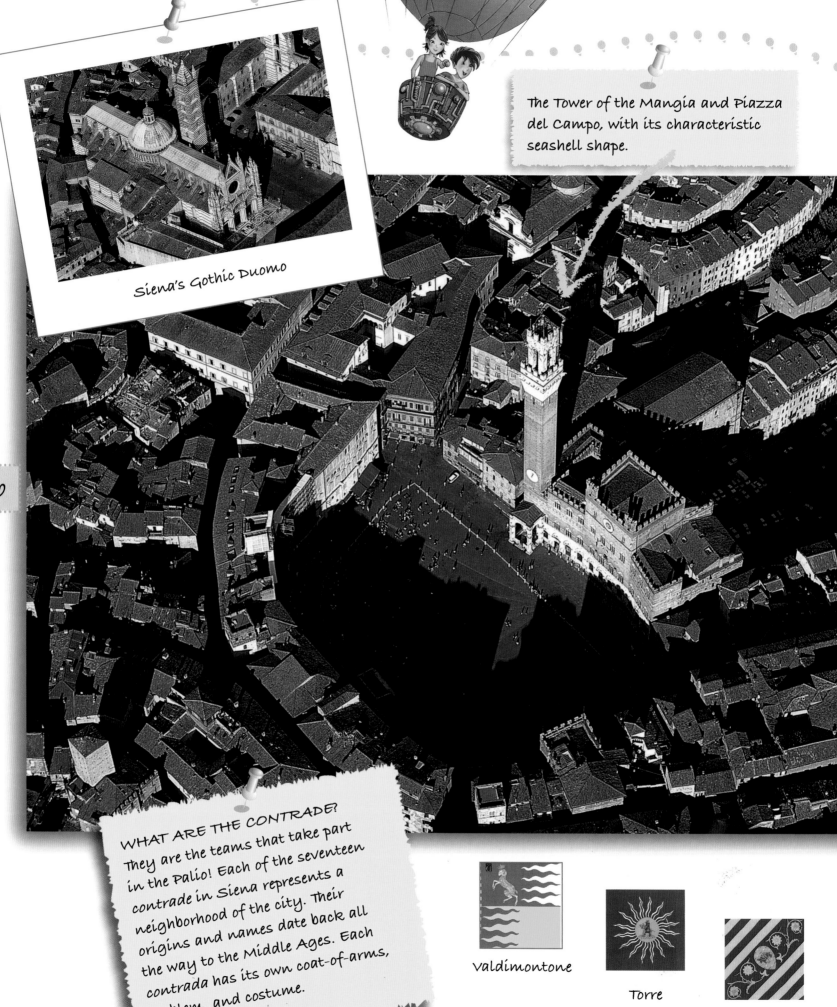

Siena's Gothic Duomo

The Tower of the Mangia and Piazza del Campo, with its characteristic seashell shape.

WHAT ARE THE CONTRADE? They are the teams that take part in the Palio! Each of the seventeen contrade in Siena represents a neighborhood of the city. Their origins and names date back all the way to the Middle Ages. Each contrada has its own coat-of-arms, emblem, and costume.

Valdimontone

Torre

Tartuca

SIENA

Aquila

Bruco

Chiocciola

Civetta

"One of the most famous squares in the world…it has a characteristic shape recalling a seashell…the famous Palio horse race is held there…"

"Alex, what are you reading?"

"I'm looking for some useful information about our next destination: Siena."

"Well, then look down! The famous seashell-shaped square is right below us! We're here! By the way, did you find any information about the Palio? I don't quite understand what it's all about," wondered Penny.

"Technically, it's a horse race, each horse representing a team, called a *contrada*. Its origins date back to the Middle Ages. The name of the race comes from the prize the winner receives—a banner, called a *palio*, which the winning team keeps until the following year, thus showering them with honor and prestige. Actually, the Palio is much more than that. It is a festival beloved by the inhabitants of Siena and features very particular rituals that extend beyond the race itself. For example, the horses are blessed in church!"

Drago

"Now, it is clearer to me! However, I've read something about this square, too. See the building towering over it? It's called the Tower of the Mangia, after the nickname of its first caretaker, Giovanni di Balduccio, who was known as 'the Mangia,' which means 'the eater,' because he was just that…a big eater!" laughed Penny. "Did you see how tall it is? It is 1132 feet from its base to its lightning rod, and to get to the top, you have to climb 503 stairs!"

Giraffa

"Gulp! I'm really happy not to have to climb all the way up there because…." Alex was interrupted by the arrival of a message on Epsilon, Jr.: "Welcome to Siena. Here's some help to find the next clue: You will find the puzzle you are looking for on the next-to-last step of the staircase that winds up to the top of the Tower of the Mangia. Happy climbing!"

"Noooo!" Alex cried, despairingly.

"Come on, Alex, look on the bright side. We don't have to climb 503 stairs…only 502," said Penny with a smile.

Istrice

Leocorno

Selva

Pantera

Onda

Oca

Nicchio

Lupa

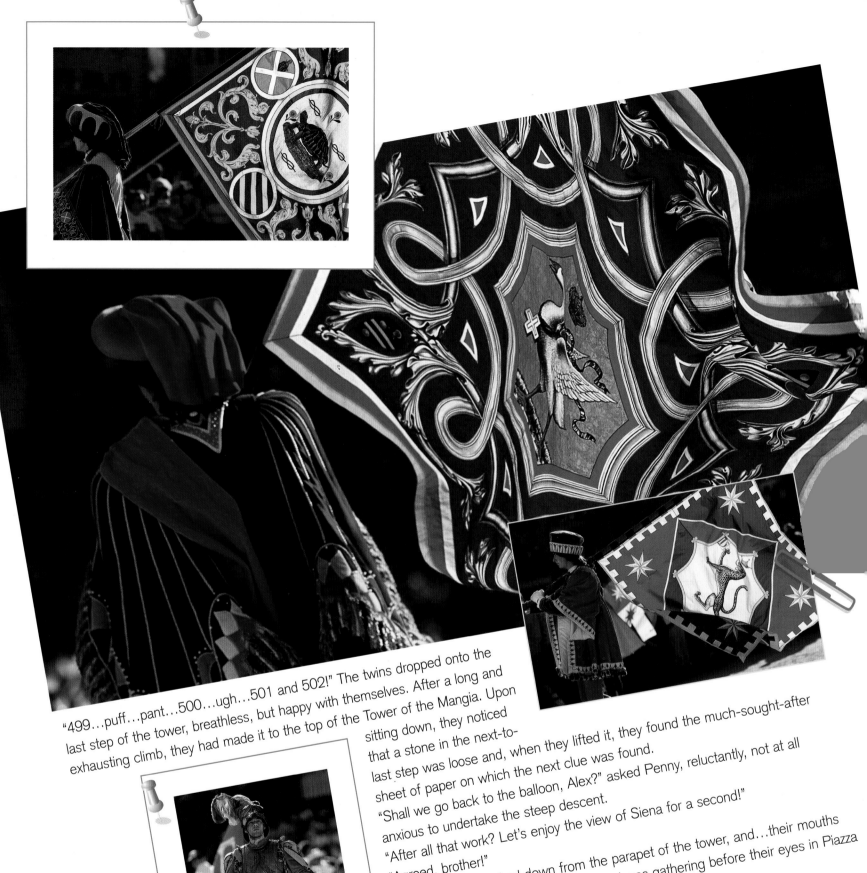

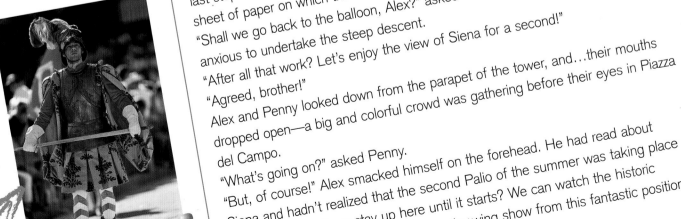

The costumes of the flag-throwers feature different colors according to the contrada they represent.

"499…puff…pant…500…ugh…501 and 502!" The twins dropped onto the last step of the tower, breathless, but happy with themselves. After a long and exhausting climb, they had made it to the top of the Tower of the Mangia. Upon sitting down, they noticed that a stone in the next-to-last step was loose and, when they lifted it, they found the much-sought-after sheet of paper on which the next clue was found.

"Shall we go back to the balloon, Alex?" asked Penny, reluctantly, not at all anxious to undertake the steep descent.

"After all that work? Let's enjoy the view of Siena for a second!"

"Agreed, brother!"

Alex and Penny looked down from the parapet of the tower, and…their mouths dropped open—a big and colorful crowd was gathering before their eyes in Piazza del Campo.

"What's going on?" asked Penny.

"But, of course!" Alex smacked himself on the forehead. He had read about Siena and hadn't realized that the second Palio of the summer was taking place today! "Why don't we stay up here until it starts? We can watch the historic parade with its costumes and the flag-throwing show from this fantastic position

DID YOU KNOW THAT…

The Palio is won by the horse that gets to the finish line—even without its rider! In this case, the winning horse is doubly celebrated and attends the winning contrada's banquet as a guest of honor.

The Tower of the Mangia

The Palio

SOLVE THIS CLUE

CONNECT THE DOTS FROM **1** TO **61** AND YOU WILL SEE THE SYMBOLIC ANIMAL OF BOTH A CONTRADA AND OF THE NEXT CITY YOU NEED TO REACH.

The Tiber was so important to the Romans, it was considered to be a god.
It was portrayed as an old bearded man that sat around, peacefully leaning against an amphora from which gushed the waters of the river.

The Castel Sant'Angelo has had a truly busy history! It was built to be the mausoleum for Emperor Hadrian, but later became a fortified castle. Today, it contains the artillery museum.

There are ten enormous statues of angels along the Sant'Angelo Bridge.

After Rhea Silvia, the only daughter of King Numitor, gave birth to two children, Romulus and Remus, Numitor's evil brother ordered one of his servants to kill the twins. However, the servant, overcome with pity, placed them in a basket and set them afloat in the Tiber River. The basket washed up on the shore, where the two crying babies attracted the attention of a she-wolf; she raised them along with her own cubs. When they grew up, the twins founded the city of Rome.

ROME

"Look, Alex, we're arriving in Rome! See that river down there? That's the Tiber, and from here you can see some of the important monuments of the city, like the Imperial Forums, a group of monumental squares where there are temples, markets, and where a good part of ancient Roman public life took place."

"*Roma caput mundi*," declared Alex, as a solemn expression came over his face.

"What?" Penny burst out laughing. "What did you say?"

"I wanted to demonstrate my perfect knowledge of Latin to you."

"Perfect knowledge? Okay, let's hear a bit. What does that phrase mean?"

"Well, it means…Rome…that is…kaput…I meant that…okay, I confess, I happened to catch that phrase written in your book, but now I'm curious. Let's see what it means."

"Here it is." Penny opened her book on Roman history. "It's a Latin proverb used to describe Rome as the capital of the world. In truth,

The Imperial Forums seen from the balloon

The Trevi Fountain

the city of Rome was the heart of the Roman Empire for centuries, which was very large and contained the majority of the lands then known. So, they really believed that Rome was the center of the world."

"Oh, sister-of-mine who knows everything," said Alex, standing like a Roman orator, "tell me the legend of the she-wolf and the birth of Rome!"

"My pleasure, brother-of-mine!" answered Penny, with an equally serious expression. "Also because it concerns two twins like us," she added, smiling.

Alex's portable computer suddenly vibrated, a sign that another message had arrived with the instructions for finding the new clue.

"Welcome to Rome. Before finding the next clue, you must visit the Colosseum and St. Peter's Basilica. To set the route on the balloon's on-board computer, carefully examine this map of Rome on which some of the city's most important monuments are shown; mark the Colosseum and St. Peter's with an 'X.' Need help? The first is an ancient Roman-era monument that looks like a stadium. The second has an enormous dome and is found at the end of a circular courtyard with an ancient Egyptian obelisk in the middle."

The floor of the Colosseum was usually covered with sand for shows, like chariot races and gladiator fights, but sometimes it was filled with water for magnificent naval battles with real ships!

In the stands, there was room for 70,000 spectators. Can you imagine how loudly they could cheer? The audience could sit in five different sections, organized according to the social class to which they belonged.

Ringside were seats occupied by top public figures like senators and a platform from which the emperor watched the games.

THE COLOSSEUM

The Colosseum is one of the most famous monuments in the world! It was the place where the Roman people attended various shows: gladiator fights, the hunt of ferocious beasts, naval battles, and chariot races. It was probably called the Colosseum because it was built near a colossal statue of the emperor Nero. The real name of this monument, however, is the Flavian Amphitheater because it was commissioned by an emperor from the Flavian Dynasty. Do you want to know the name of this emperor? Solve this puzzle by matching the letters with their corresponding symbols and filling in the blank boxes with the correct letters.

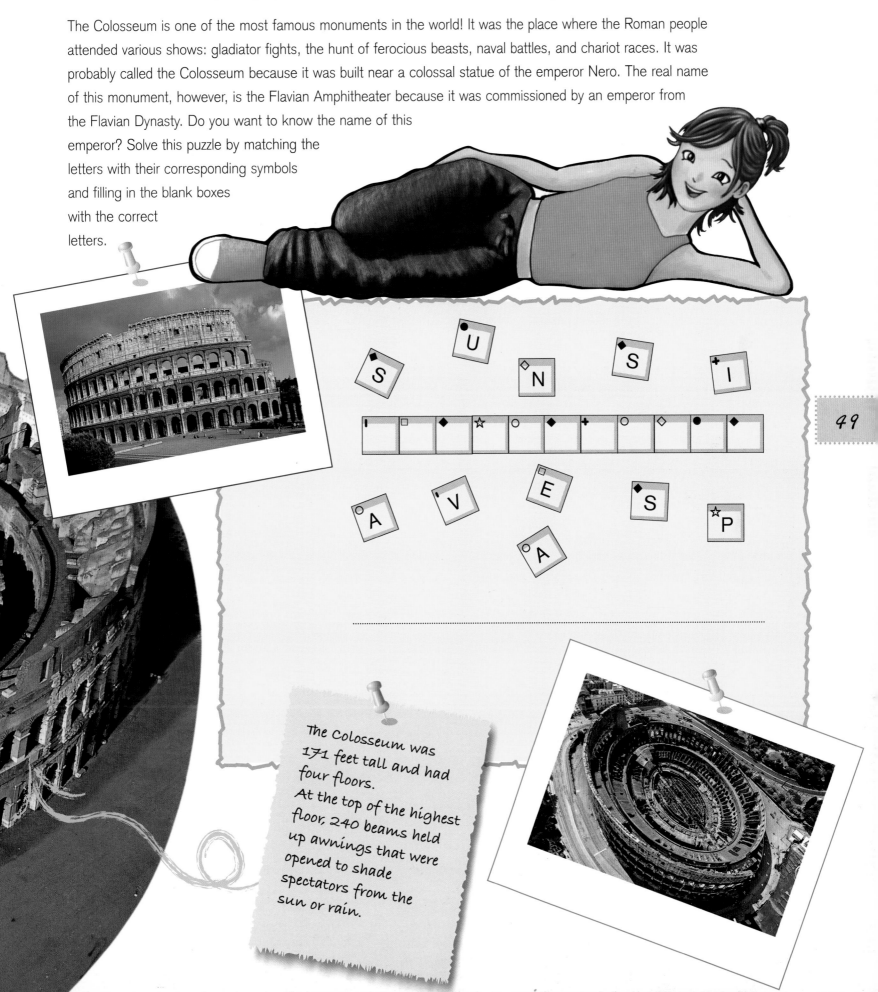

The Colosseum was 171 feet tall and had four floors.
At the top of the highest floor, 240 beams held up awnings that were opened to shade spectators from the sun or rain.

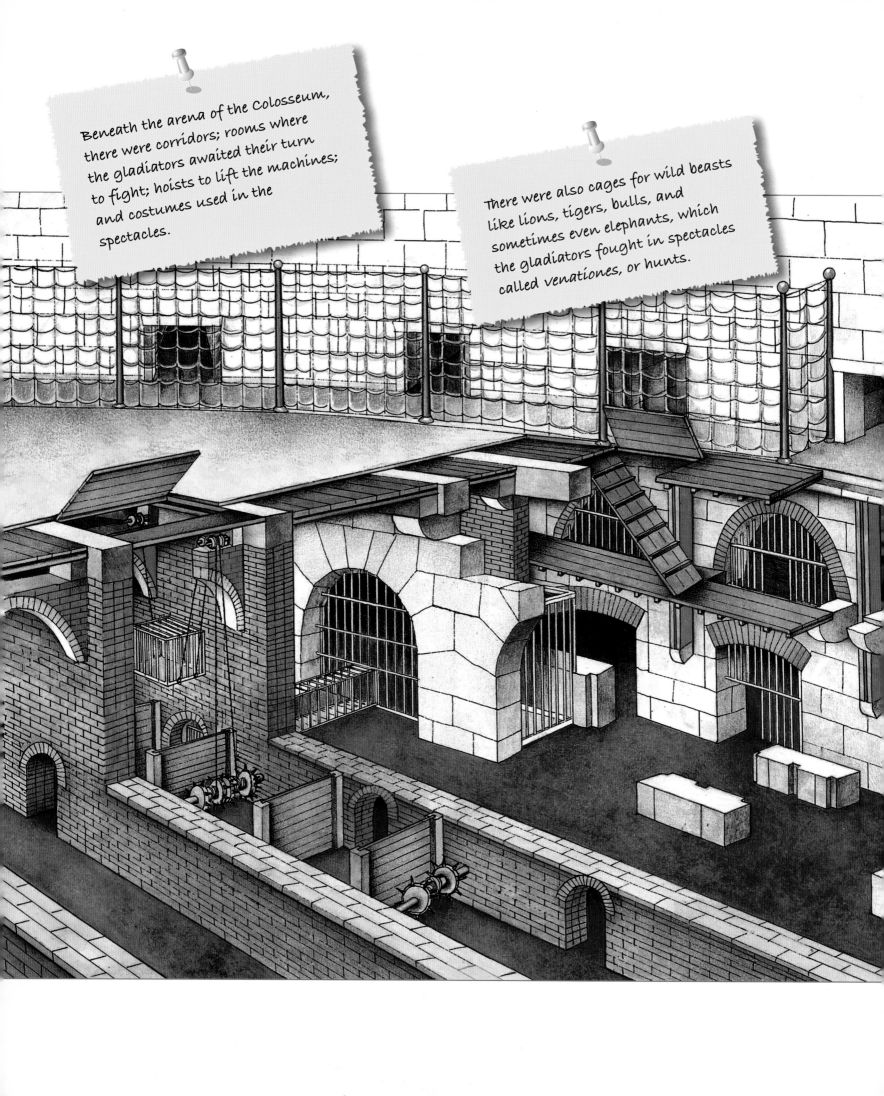

Beneath the arena of the Colosseum, there were corridors; rooms where the gladiators awaited their turn to fight; hoists to lift the machines and costumes used in the spectacles.

There were also cages for wild beasts like lions, tigers, bulls, and sometimes even elephants, which the gladiators fought in spectacles called venationes, or hunts.

GLADIATORS

The word "gladiator" comes from the name of the Roman sword called a gladius. Actually, the fighters used different types of weapons according to which they were divided into categories and called different names: the retiarius fought with a net and a trident, the Thracians with a small, round or square shield and a dagger; the Samnites wore heavy armor; and the Mirmillones used a scythe, a helmet with a fish on the crest, and a small shield.

The gladiators were usually chosen from among slaves and prisoners of war. Winners of the fights received prizes in money and the prestigious Golden Palm, and, after having won more than ten encounters, they earned their freedom from slavery.

A gladiator's bronze helmet

Gladiators in an ancient mosaic

DID YOU KNOW THAT...
In ancient Rome, the gladiator games were hugely popular. Many of the strongest fighters became celebrities, and their fights were closely followed by fan clubs.

The fighters lived and trained in the Ludus Magnus, a school for gladiators, the biggest in ancient Rome, located just a few yards from the Colosseum.

Gladiator battles were even commemorated with little terracotta statues

"Look, Penny! We are flying over St. Peter's Basilica. This church sure is big!"

"It is the biggest church in Christianity, Alex! And, it's also the oldest. The first basilica was built by Emperor Constantine in the fourth century A.D." cited Penny as she put down the guide to Rome that she had been reading until that moment. "Did you notice the dome?"

"Did I notice it? It's sure hard to miss. It's enormous," gasped Alex.

"An old acquaintance of ours designed it…"

"Who?" asked Alex.

"Do you remember the *David*, the statue that we saw in Florence?"

"Michelangelo?!"

"Right! He worked in Rome for the Pope for many years, and below us, within a few hundred yards, there are three of his most famous masterpieces," explained Penny.

"The dome is the first…but the others?"

"Have you ever heard of the statue the *Pietà* and the frescoes in the Sistine Chapel?"

"Wow!" exclaimed Alex, truly impressed. "That Michelangelo sure was a genius!"

The computer in Alex's pocket suddenly started to vibrate, indicating the arrival of a message. "Congratulations, twins. You have proven great skill in reaching the two objectives that we gave you—the Colosseum and St. Peter's. Now, I can reveal where the next clue is hidden. It is found inside the Mouth of Truth."

"The Mouth of Truth?" Alex shook his head. "Penny, I've got a really bad feeling about this!"

52

From 1508 to 1512: It took Michelangelo more than four years of constant work to fresco the more than 8,600 square feet of the Sistine Chapel vault. He painted 300 different characters. The most famous scene? The Creation of Adam.

From the window of his office, the Pope looks out to bless the crowd awaiting him in the square below.

The Pietà

Michelangelo sculpted the Pietà when he was only 23 years old! It is also the only statue that bears his signature. When he overheard another sculptor boast about being the creator of the masterpiece, Michelangelo, furious, decided to chisel his name on the section across the bosom of the Virgin Mary.

MICHELANGELO, WHAT A GENIUS!

SUBSTITUTE EACH NUMBER WITH THE CORRESPONDING LETTER OF THE ALPHABET (SEE EXAMPLES, BELOW) AND YOU WILL DISCOVER MICHELANGELO'S MYRIAD TALENTS...

A = 1   C = 3
B = 2   D = ...

1 18 3 8 9 20 5 3 20

_ _ _ _ _ _ _ _ _

19 3 21 12 16 20 15 18

_ _ _ _ _ _ _ _

16 1 9 14 20 5 18

_ _ _ _ _ _ _

THE LEGEND OF THE MOUTH OF TRUTH

Under the portico of the church of Santa Maria in Cosmedin is one of the most mysterious objects from the ancient world—a marble mask portraying the face of a river god. There are many theories concerning the purpose of this big face in ancient times. Some scholars believe that water from a fountain flowed out of the gaping mouth of the god. Others think it was an ancient manhole cover, which collected rainwater and directed it to the Cloaca Maxima, one of the biggest sewer systems in ancient Rome. Yet another view is that this big stone was the cover to a sacred well upon which vows were made. Perhaps the name, the "Mouth of Truth" comes from this ancient use, as well as a legend: Supposedly, the mouth will snap closed over the hand of a liar, breaking off his or her fingers as punishment for lying!

The twins arrived at the circle of stone inside which the clue was found. The atmosphere was not very reassuring; immersed in shadows, the Mouth of Truth seemed to be watching them, following their every move.

"Go on, Alex," ordered Penny. "The clue is there inside the mouth. Put your hand in and pull it out."

"No!"

"Alex, we don't have time for this! Come on!"

"No, no, no! You put *your* hand in there!" Alex peeked into the opening of the mouth. It was deep and black. Who knew what was hiding in there, not that he believed in that absurd legend, but…

"Your arms are longer than mine, so only you can reach the clue! Wait a second," said Penny with a little ironic smile. "I know what the problem is! You're afraid that the mouth is going to snap shut!"

"Me? No! I don't believe in that old legend, plus I don't lie! Well, almost never," stammered Alex.

"Okay! Prove it! Put your hand in there!"

"Geez!" Despite himself, Alex slowly inserted his hand into the mouth, and then his arm, all the way up to his shoulder, and then suddenly, he started to yell, "Peeeeenyyyyyy!"

"What?! Alex! What's the matter? Alex, did it bite you? I'll help! Wait…" but Alex's laughter interrupted her.

"You fell for it! I got you!"

"Alex!"

SOLVE THIS CLUE

HELP ALEX AND PENNY SET THE CORRECT COURSE ON THE ON-BOARD COMPUTER BY CHOOSING THE RIGHT ROUTE THROUGH THE LETTERS TO GET TO…

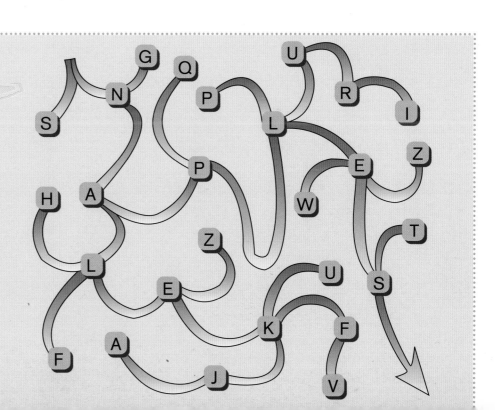

SARDINIA

After reading the instructions left by K for the third time, Alex had no more doubts. He could fly Epsilon by himself, and he couldn't wait to try. He glanced quickly at Penny, who was absorbed in her book, *Naples: Traditions and Legends*, then he gripped the joystick, turned off the automatic pilot, and pushed the accelerator down. For a drawn-out moment, nothing happened, and then…the unexpected! The balloon shot off at a supersonic speed toward the open sea, flipping everything in the cabin over, including the twins.

"Aaaaleeeex! I'll…" but Alex didn't hear what his sister was yelling because the wind was thundering so loudly that any other sounds were drowned out! There was only one thing to do—Alex pulled out the Epsilon, Jr. and nervously contacted K. A few seconds later, the young inventor's answer came, but it was much different from what Alex expected. "That's great news! The rotating turbine engines were just a prototype. I'm thrilled to know that they work! Now, however, we will have to reprogram the on-board computer from here, which will take a couple hours. You're lucky. According to my calculations, you have reached Sardinia, one of the most beautiful islands in the world. Wait there until Epsilon is ready to take off again for Naples. You will arrive in four seconds…three…two…one….Now!" The balloon suddenly stopped, and the twins slowly stuck their heads out of the cabin to see—amazed and relieved—white beaches and blue sea below them. Alex turned to Penny and barely managed to refrain from laughing; his sister's ponytail had been twisted by the wind and now hung over one of her eyes…a very angry eye! "Have you seen where I brought you, Penny? The sea of Sardinia is famous for being crystal clear. You can see all the little fish without using a mask, aren't you happy?"

"Hmmmph!"

GUESS WHAT

Sea animal is hiding behind this rock. Do you want a hint? Connect the dots from 1 to 77 and it will appear.

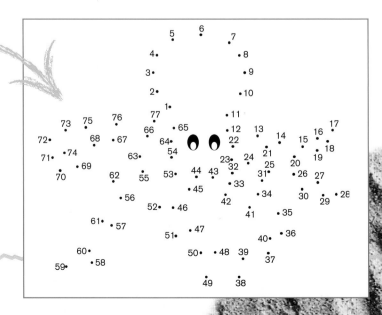

This little strip of a beach in Sardinia seen from the balloon is blinding white!

Flamingos come to Sardinia in September before migrating south for the winter.

DID YOU KNOW THAT...

In northern Sardinia, the beach of Budelli is famous because its sand is pink! The color is due to tiny bits of coral that are washed onto the beach by the waves.

The pink beach of Budelli

SEA QUIZ

While waiting for Epsilon to be ready for departure, answer the questions on the quiz and check how much you know about the marine world.

On the opposite page, use the color corresponding to the correct answer for each question to fill in the numbered spaces. When you have finished the drawing, a very rare marine animal that lives in Sardinia will be revealed to you.

1. IT LOOKS LIKE A HARMLESS LITTLE UMBRELLA BUT IF YOU TOUCH IT, IT WILL STING YOU. IT IS:

an octopus

a jellyfish

a starfish

2. A DOLPHIN IS A:

mollusk

fish

mammal

3. THE SEAHORSE IS ALSO CALLED A:

Hippodrome

Hippocampus

hippopotamus

4. CORAL IS:

a plant

a rock

an animal

5. THE BLUE WHALE IS THE BIGGEST ANIMAL ON THE PLANET. IT CAN BE AS LONG AS:

40 feet

100 feet

170 feet

6. POSIDONIA IS

a fish

a shell

an algae

7. THE MOLLUSK THAT DEFENDS ITSELF BY SPRAYING INK IS:

a clam

a squid

a mussel

8. SEA TURTLES LIVE A VERY LONG TIME! JUST IMAGINE THAT A TURTLE CAN LIVE UP TO:

20 years

50 years

100 years

59

NAPLES

"By now, we should be back on track," said Alex, after having consulted the balloon's computer, "and be close to our next stop."

"Neapolis," murmured Penny, without taking her eyes off the big guidebook she was consulting.

"What did you say, Penny?"

"Neapolis is the ancient name of Naples. That's what it was called."

"Let me guess, the Romans were involved. The Romans were always involved."

"Nope! It's a Greek name. Neos means 'new,' and polis means 'city,' so it means 'new city.' The Ancient Greeks called it that to distinguish it from the old city, where they had been living for years."

"Wow, how creative!"

"Basically. But since then, Naples has become the land of creativity. The city's history goes back thousands of years. Its inhabitants are famous for their hospitality and enthusiasm."

"And do you think they would be so hospitable as to offer us a pizza?"

"Alex, that's a fantastic idea! I'm hungry! Let's land and find a pizzeria. In the meantime, I'll tell you how pizza was born."

"Finally, an interesting story," Alex answered, snickering.

Castel dell'Ovo

DID YOU KNOW THAT...

Pizza has an ancient history, but in Naples, they say that the traditional recipe made from dough, tomato, and mozzarella was created by a young pizza maker who prepared it for Queen Margherita of Savoy, who was visiting the city. She liked the pizza so much that she gave it her name. That is the story of Pizza Margherita.

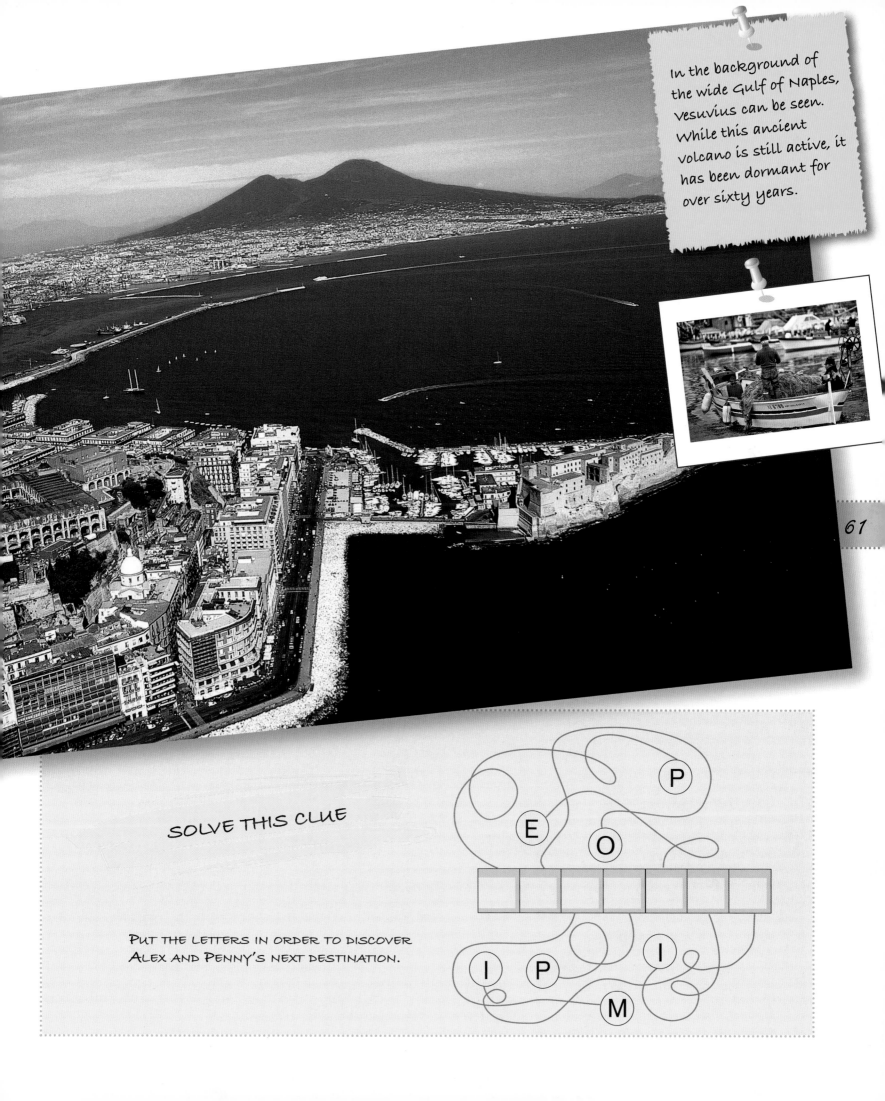

In the background of the wide Gulf of Naples, Vesuvius can be seen. While this ancient volcano is still active, it has been dormant for over sixty years.

SOLVE THIS CLUE

PUT THE LETTERS IN ORDER TO DISCOVER ALEX AND PENNY'S NEXT DESTINATION.

P E O I P M I

POMPEII

"Hey, Penny. That's Vesuvius over there, isn't it?" asked Alex, pointing at the mountain he saw in the distance.

"Yes, and the city you see below us is Pompeii."

Alex remembered having heard that name before. "It's a very famous place, right? But, why?"

"Well, it's kind of a sad story," answered Penny. "Pompeii is famous because it was buried by an eruption of the Vesuvius volcano."

"What? An eruption?" asked Alex.

"Yes! Imagine it's morning on a summer day like any other, but in the year A.D. 79. The city of Pompeii wakes up and starts its daily life. Kids are going to school, the first deals are made in the market of the forum, the shops open, goods are unloaded from ships in the port, and the first customers enter the thermal baths. Suddenly, there is a huge boom and stones and poisonous gases from Vesuvius start to rain down on the city. The Pompeiians try to take shelter in their houses and flee, but the eruption is incredibly violent. A final discharge of gases and burning ash cover the city, enveloping everything, without leaving any chance of escape."

Pompeii was one of the most extraordinary archaeological discoveries of all time. But did you know that it was found by accident? In 1748, a farmer who was digging a hole in his vineyard unearthed the first work of art from the buried city.

The streets of Pompeii were very colorful. The shops faced them with brightly painted signs and inscriptions; announcements and ancient advertisements were painted directly onto the walls!

"Man! That's awful," said Alex, deeply impressed.

"Yeah! And the second reason Pompeii is famous is that its sudden and violent end caused the city to be embalmed, basically; when the archaeologists started to excavate, they discovered that the ash had preserved it perfectly. Therefore, today it can be seen and visited—all the shops, the houses…it feels just like going back in time."

The Roman domus were the most luxurious houses and had several rooms. This is the atrium, a central room located just past the entrance. The pool you see in the middle was used to collect rainwater.

The walls of the domus were embellished with colorful frescoes illustrating nature scenes or characters from ancient Roman myths.

At the end of the atrium, there was the tablinum, the room where the owner of the house had his office and received guests.

The bedrooms looked onto the peristylium, a big garden lined with porticoes and decorated with statues or little fountains.

The twins set out along the main street of the city, proceeding to explore Pompeii. Alex was fascinated by the atmosphere in the streets. He would never have admitted to Penny that he was interested in something historical, that was for sure, but he couldn't help but be amazed by everything. It was as if he had jumped back in time two thousand years. The feeling intensified when they decided to visit the inside of a few houses. Alex had always imagined that the ancient world was the plain color of white marble, but he was now discovering that it was actually quite colorful thanks to the brightly painted frescoes and mosaics. One mosaic in particular made him laugh—it portrayed a dog with a ferocious expression and the words "Cave Canem," or in other words, as they read in Penny's guide, "Beware of Dog!"

Epsilon, Jr. vibrated in Alex's hands as a new message arrived. "It is time to move on. Here is the puzzle you must solve."

SOLVE THIS CLUE

IN THE STRING OF LETTERS BELOW, CROSS OUT THE LETTERS THAT MAKE UP THESE COMMON POMPEII WORDS. READ THE REMAINING LETTERS TO DISCOVER ALEX AND PENNY'S NEXT DESTINATION.
VESUVIUS - DOMUS - ERUPTION - FRESCOES

65

VETSHUVEIUSDOVMOUSLERUCPTANOIONETFRNESCAOES

TAORMINA

"Alex, do you think you can modify Epsilon's route a little?" The request was made in a very soft voice, but it had the same effect on Alex as a thunderbolt!

"What? What did I hear? My sister suggesting that I break the rules and turn off the autopilot?!"

"Well, no, I wouldn't say that. It's just that we are flying over Taormina, which has one of the best-preserved ancient Greek amphitheaters in Sicily. Do you remember reading that book of ancient Greek comedies? It would be great to see where they would have been performed."

"I remember! And relax; the scheduled route passes right over Taormina. There is your theater!" Penny turned just in time to see the balloon approach the hill where the theater was located.

"Do you know what else I remember?" added Alex, "You got furious when you found out that women were not allowed to act in ancient times!"

"Does that seem fair to you? Actors wore masks that covered their faces, allowing them to interpret any part, even those of women. The masks amplified their voices, like modern microphones. Part of their costumes were also composed of long togas, which had different colors depending on the emotions of the character, and by objects that helped the public to identify them immediately, like a sword for a soldier or a cane for the elderly."

"And, if I remember well, there were also musicians, right?" asked Alex.

"Yes! Music was very important because some parts were sung. As a matter of fact, the part of the theater between the stage and the audience was called the orchestra. Why do you remember all those details so well?" Penny asked, amazed by Alex's unusual interest in things that he usually called "old stuff."

"You have been muttering those stories about old stuff in my ears for years...I tried not to listen, but something stuck all the same," snickered Alex, as he ducked to avoid the huge book Penny threw at him.

The ancient Greek amphitheater was built on a hill overlooking the coast.

The stage was the part of the theater where the shows took place. It was also the place where the "special-effects" machines were located, like instruments to produce sound or lighting effects and pulleys to make the actors playing gods fly!

This is the cavea, or the part of the theater for the audience. It featured perfect acoustics, which made it possible to hear the show even from seats in the rows furthest from the stage.

THE VOLCANO ETNA

"Wow! It sure is impressive!," whispered Alex.

"Yeah! It really *is* impressive," repeated Penny, softly.

The balloon was slowly approaching the volcano Etna, and the twins started to feel a bit frightened by the massive body of the mountain and the sight of the craters on its top.

"Alex, you said that Etna is an active volcano, didn't you?" asked Penny without taking her eyes off the spectacle of the volcano.

"Very active! I read on the Internet that the last eruption was in 2002."

"How tall is it?"

"It is about 11,000 feet, but it's difficult to know for sure, Penny, because with each eruption the volcano's height changes. Just think, there once was a gulf here which slowly, eruption after eruption, filled with hardened lava that over the course of thousands of years piled up to this height! Currently, there are four craters at the top of the volcano, but even that isn't a definite number. New ones could open up at the next eruption."

"That's not terribly reassuring news, Alex. Do we have to land right here?"

A message made Alex's computer vibrate.

"Don't be afraid. Land here and follow the directions that will appear on the screen of the on-board computer. Your destination is very close!"

Etna's eruptions are spectacular—following a series of explosions, fountains of lava flow from the craters at the top of the volcano.

Etna's main crater is the oldest of the four on its top, and it has a diameter of about two miles.

In addition to the four biggest craters, there are many other openings in the volcano's crust from which plumes of smoke constantly puff.

Proving that he knew how to land perfectly, Alex delicately settled the balloon onto a small spur of rock. Now, the only thing left to do was to read the message that had appeared on the computer screen.

"You have one last puzzle to tackle. Solve these encoded problems and type in the result on the computer's keyboard. Only the exact sequence of numbers will allow you to read the next message containing directions to the Agency's General Headquarters. How are your mathematics skills?"

"Math!" exclaimed Penny with an expression of deep disgust on her face. "I hate math!"

"Don't worry, sis! We'll still be able to break the code!"

◀■▶ = 12   ■ = 10   ▶▶ = 6   ▲≋▼ = 7

◀■▶ − ■ = ◀▶   ◀▶ = _____

◀▶ + ▶▶ = ▶▶◀◀   ▶▶◀◀ = _____

▲▼ + ▶▶◀◀ = ◀□▶   ◀□▶ = _____

◀□▶ − ▶▶ = ⬝◼   ⬝◼ = _____

"Get out of the balloon and take the path on your right. You'll come to a cavern. Enter it, and when you are asked for a password, answer 'WS.'"

"Penny, what does that mean?" They had followed the instructions and now they were standing in front of a narrow crevice between two big volcanic rocks behind which opened a small and dark cavern.

"It means that the mysteries are not over! Let's go in! The twins grabbed hands and, taking deep breaths, poked through the opening. Their eyes took a few seconds to adjust to the dark, and the first things that Alex and Penny managed to see were the low ceiling from which hung some stubby stalactites and the damp rock walls surrounding a space no bigger than their bedroom. Without doubt, there was nobody in that cave.

"And now?" asked Penny. "Who's going to ask us for the password?"

"There must be some trick," Alex said, "a trapdoor or some device to alert them to our presence." The twins glanced at each other and started to explore the cave by feeling the damp rock walls.

"It's probably something indistinguishable like one of those stalactites or one of those tufts of moss or…"

"Or what? What were you going to say, Alex?"

"Or…that telephone over there."

Penny turned skeptically, only to see what Alex was pointing at: a telephone, there was no doubt about it, with a long cord that disappeared into the rock! The twins quickly lifted the receiver. In an uncertain tone of voice, Alex asked, "hello?"

"Hello, who's speaking?" answered a woman's voice.

"Well, um, it's Alex and Penny."

"Password, please."

"WS."

"Access granted. Please await complete opening."

"Hey, just a second," asked the twins, "opening of what?" But they didn't have time to finish their sentence. The walls at the back of the cavern started to vibrate and then shake violently and finally…to roll up right into the ceiling! Bright light began to filter down from the crack that was opening up. Having adjusted to the darkness in the cave, the twins couldn't make out the silhouettes coming toward them with the light at their backs, but they clearly saw a pair of big black-and-white shoes and heard a deep, polite voice declare, "Welcome! You did it! You have reached the General Headquarters of the WS, the World Secret, the only worldwide secret agency for the investigation of mysteries! Come along, come in, and I will explain everything to you!" Holding hands, the twins gathered their courage and crossed the stone threshold.

The spectacle that opened right in front of their eyes left them speechless—a wide room, so big that they were unable to see either to the back of it or up to its ceiling. It had been dug right out of the rock of the volcano. Even though it was underground, it wasn't at all dark or damp like the cavern through which they had entered, because the golden light that moments before had blinded them, now was spreading warm sunlight throughout the cave. Furthermore, every inch of rock had been lined with electronic panels and equipment right out of a science-fiction film. Dozens of agents wearing long white lab coats were working frenetically around the computers, inputting data and checking the results of their research. Others were assembling strange objects, the function of which the twins couldn't even imagine. Watching them work, Alex immediately thought about the loony Agent K.

"You have to admit that seeing our computer room makes a certain impression. Alex, what do you think?"

Alex stuttered in a soft voice, without taking his eyes off the room, "Out of this world! Mega-galactic! It's absolutely incredible! There are computers everywhere!"

"Well, I'm happy that you like our little technological toys, and I think you'll be able to use them soon. And you, young lady, do you have anything to say?"

"I'm…speechless," answered Penny. "It's a truly impressive sight, but I was wondering, well, what are we looking at exactly?"

"Right! And, who are you?"

The twins turned around to catch the ironic and cheerful gaze of the man who had invited them to come in. Now, they could see him clearly from those funny black-and-white shoes to his long, white, and perfectly groomed mustache and goatee, which contrasted with his rebellious and uncombed hair in two wispy tufts at the sides of his face.

"You are right. It is time for answers not questions. First of all, let me introduce myself. I'm Cornelius Misterius and I am the general director of the World Secret, which, as I said, is a secret agency with the duty to investigate unsolved mysteries around the world. Do you know about the Bermuda Triangle or the disappearance of the dinosaurs? Those are the last cases we dealt with. This is our job and also yours," added Cornelius Misterius with a sparkle in his eye, "if you are still interested in…"

"But, of course! Certainly! Absolutely! Yesssssss!" answered the twins in unison. "When do we start? What will we do? What mission will we go on?"

"What enthusiasm," smiled Cornelius Misterius. "We will contact you soon. Something's up in Egypt…we will see…but now, one thing is missing. Here…your badges! Now you are officially special agents of the

WORLD SECRET!

WE COULD NEVER HAVE DONE IT

WITHOUT YOUR HELP!!!

DO YOU WANT TO COME WITH US ON OUR NEXT ADVENTURE?

THEN TAKE YOUR BADGE AND YOU WILL BE AN AGENT OF THE WORLD SECRET, TOO!

www.alexepenny.it

SOLUTIONS

PAGE 16

PAGE 17

M	O	U	S	E
I	N	T	E	R
L	I	G	H	T
A	L	O	U	D
N	E	V	E	R

PAGE 21

PAGE 21

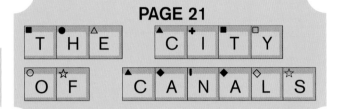

PAGES 24-25

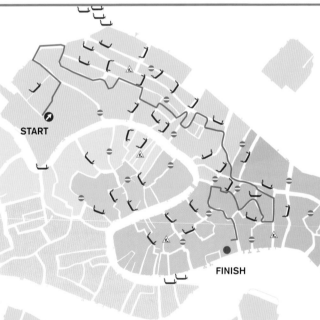

PAGES 26-27

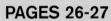

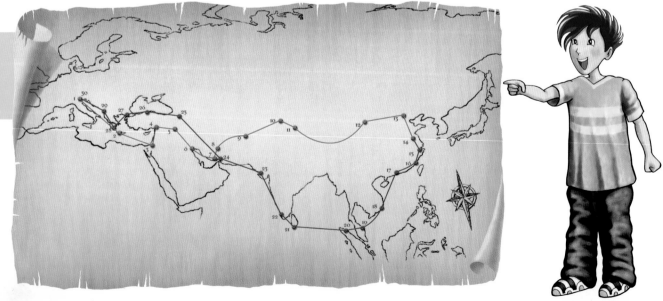

PAGE 29

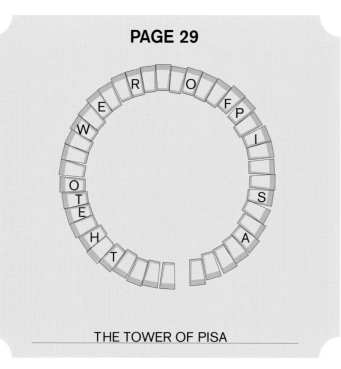

THE TOWER OF PISA

PAGE 33

PAGE 33

the first is the sixth letter of the alphabet F

the second is the second letter in "Alex" L

the third is in both "hot" and "cold" but not "warm" O

the fourth is in "roar" twice, in "roll" once, and never in "goal" R

the fifth is the same as the last E

the sixth is the third letter in "Penny" N

the seventh is the third letter in the alphabet C

the eighth is in both "Alex" and "Penny" E

PAGES 36-37

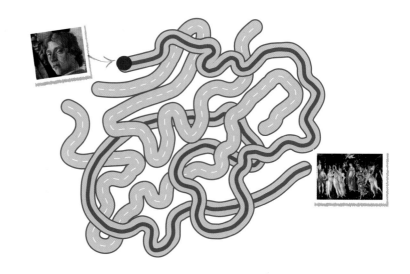

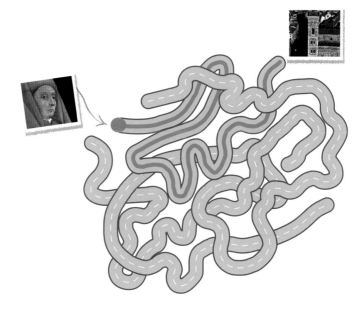

PAGE 39

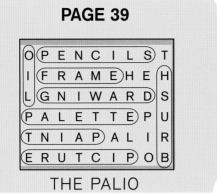

```
O P E N C I L S T
I F R A M E H E H
L G N I W A R D S
P A L E T T E P U
T N I A P A L I R
E R U T C I P O B
```

THE PALIO

PAGE 43

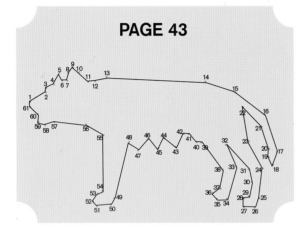

PAGES 46-47

PAGE 49

PAGE 53

1	18	3	8	9	20	5	3	20
A	R	C	H	I	T	E	C	T

19	3	21	12	16	20	15	18
S	C	U	L	P	T	O	R

16	1	9	14	20	5	18
P	A	I	N	T	E	R

PAGE 55

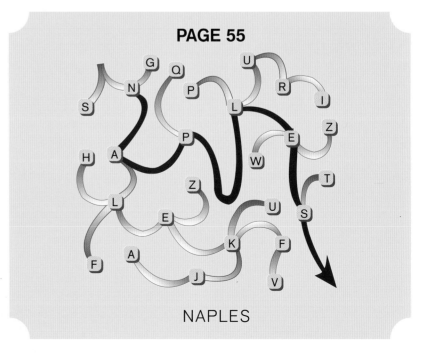

NAPLES

PAGE 56

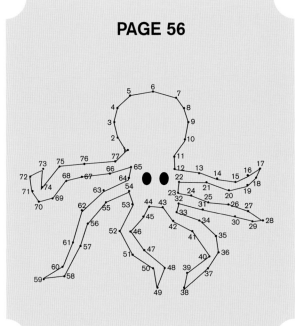

PAGES 58-59

1. Jellyfish have tentacles that cause redness and welts if they touch the skin. **2.** Though they look like fish, dolphins are actually mammals like us, and they have calves instead of laying eggs like fish do. **3.**The seahorse belongs to the genus known as Hippocampus. A hippopotamus is a large African mammal, and the Hippodrome was an ancient Roman arena for equestrian events. **4.** Coral is an animal. The hard part we see is formed by the skeletons of tiny animals that look like tiny octopuses. They eat plankton. **5.** Blue whales grow to about 100 feet long. **6.** Posidonia is a type of algae. **7.** When it senses danger, squid squirts ink on its enemy and takes advantage of its predator's confusion to escape. **8.** Although it is very difficult to establish the age of a turtle, we know that some specimens have lived at least one hundred years!

PAGE 61

PAGE 65

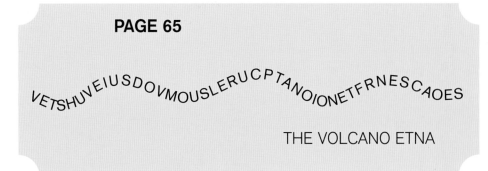

THE VOLCANO ETNA

PAGE 70

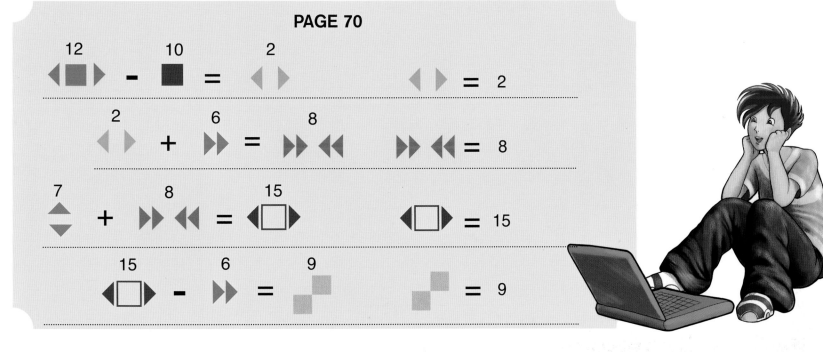

AUTHOR: GIADA FRANCIA

translator: AMY EZRIN

graphic designer: PATRIZIA BALOCCO LOVISETTI

illustrator: ANGELO COLOMBO

PHOTO CREDITS

© 2006 White Star S.p.A.
Via Candido Sassone, 22/24
13100 Vercelli, Italy
www.whitestar.it

ISBN-10: 88-544-0160-9
ISBN 13: 978-88-544-0160-0

Reprints:
1 2 3 4 5 6   10 09 08 07 06

Printed in India
Color separation by: Fotomec, Turin, Italy